# DOWN LILAC LANE

In 1942, Viney Lucas and her brothers were taken by their mother to live in their grandmother's cottage in Lilac Lane in Wales. A lasting friendship began when Sybil came to live with them. After her father returned home from the war, Viney became tied to caring for him and her brothers, whilst Sybil was free to pursue the nursing career they had both dreamed of. Yet the bonds forged between them growing up in Lilac Lane never weakened.

*Books by Catriona McCuaig*
*in the Linford Romance Library:*

ICE MAIDEN
MAIL ORDER BRIDE
OUT OF THE SHADOWS
ROMANY ROSE

CATRIONA McCUAIG

# DOWN LILAC LANE

*Complete and Unabridged*

**LINFORD**
*Leicester*

First published in Great Britain in 2006

First Linford Edition
published 2007

British Library CIP Data

McCuaig, Catriona
   Down Lilac Lane.—Large print ed.—
Linford romance library
1. Love stories
2. Large type books
I. Title
823.9′2 [F]

ISBN 978–1–84617–796–5

Published by
F. A. Thorpe (Publishing)
Anstey, Leicestershire

Set by Words & Graphics Ltd.
Anstey, Leicestershire
Printed and bound in Great Britain by
T. J. International Ltd., Padstow, Cornwall

This book is printed on acid-free paper

# Looking Back . . .

Looking back on her life from the great age of twenty-two, Viney Lucas could see that everything that had happened to her to date had its roots in the summer of 1942. That was the year they had gone to live in Wales, when her father had disappeared from their lives, and when she had met Sybil Waite who was to become a lifelong friend.

In the way of all children, she hadn't questioned these events very deeply at the time. Although miserable about her father, she accepted the fact of his absence as part of the way things were, along with the frequent air-raids, the shortage of food, and having to carry gas-masks to school. It was her mother, Laura, who bore the brunt of keeping the family safe in a world which seemed to have gone mad.

Laura's neighbour, Dorothy Brewster, listened sympathetically to her friend's fears. The two families shared an Anderson shelter whenever the air-raid sirens went and they had to hurry down the garden in the middle of the night.

'You say that your Neil wants you to go to Wales to his mother. If you're determined to stay here, why not send the kiddies? I'm sure she'd love to have them.'

Laura shook her head. 'She's eighty years old, Dot. I couldn't wish this lot on her. They're a lively lot, and young John can be a real handful at times. Well, what two-year-old isn't?'

'Eighty! Are you sure? She must have been getting on a bit when she had Neil, then.'

'Forty-two. They were married for a good many years with no sign of a baby, and they'd given up hope when Marion finally appeared.'

'That's Neil's married sister in Australia, isn't it?' Dorothy recalled.

'That's right. Then Neil came along two years later and that was the family they'd always longed for.'

'Sad, then, when you think about it — Marion so far away and Neil mixed up in this war. It might be a comfort to the poor old soul if you did go down to Llan-whatsit.'

'I might go down for a holiday, and then we'll see,' Laura mused at the time, but what with one thing and another, she never did get organised. With four young children there was always so much to do, what with queuing for rations and washing and mending and all the other things a mother has to do, war or no war.

She did, of course, write the occasional letter to old Mrs Lucas, and always received an answer by return of post, written in the beautiful copperplate handwriting which everyone of her generation had been taught at school.

Then one morning she was surprised to find the vicar on her doorstep, looking solemn. Her first thought was 'Neil!' and for a moment she thought she was going to pass out, but then she realised that if anything had happened to him it would have been the telegraph boy standing there, clutching an ominous orange envelope, not Charles Frobisher with his hat in his hands.

'I'm sorry the children weren't at Sunday School last week,' she began. 'Mark had a cold and I thought it best to keep them home.'

'It's not that. I'm afraid I'm the bearer of bad news,' he murmured, and she knew at once that Emily Lucas had passed away.

She ushered him in and closed the door.

'I had a phone call from Carmarthenshire this morning, Mrs Lucas, from my opposite number in your mother-in-law's village. The operator was unable to find a number for you, but of course you're not on the phone here. Mrs Lucas never missed a communion service, so when she failed to appear at the eight o'clock service he became worried and asked his wife to call round. She found the key hidden under the mat and let herself in, and found Mrs Lucas dead in bed.'

Laura put her hand to her mouth, blinking back the tears.

'It was all very peaceful, I'm told,' he went on. 'She must have passed away in her sleep. Well, she'd had a good long life and a quiet end at the last. Could any of us wish for more?'

They sat without speaking for a few moments, each lost in their own thoughts.

'She was fortunate, wasn't she?' Laura said at last. 'I mean, when you think about all those poor people being killed in air-raids, or losing family members because of that man Hitler . . . ' Her voice trailed off as she thought of her husband, so far away from home and soon to be in the thick of the fighting.

Later, she called to see Dorothy who was as welcoming as ever.

'Of course I'll take the little ones while you're away, dear. I'll be only too glad to help. I'll have the boys, too, if you like.'

'No, they're coming with me, Dot. I think they're old enough to attend a funeral, and Matthew's quite proud to think he'll be representing his dad there. What with Neil being on active service, and Marion over in Australia, we're the only family she has in Britain at the moment.'

The boys were thrilled at the prospect of a train journey and as they had only met 'Gran' on one occasion, they were in high spirits when they left for Wales, which left Laura in peace to contemplate their future without Neil's mother in their lives.

\* \* \*

Llanidris was either a village or a hamlet, depending on whether you took into account the country lanes and the big estate which lay close to its borders.

Postal officials from outside the country were constantly confusing it with the many other places whose names began with Llan, a word which had originally described a monastic enclosure back in the sixth century.

'They wouldn't have this problem if they learned to speak good Welsh,' the local postmistress grumbled, when explaining matters to Laura after the funeral. 'People getting evacuated from England wanting letters sent to them. Ah, well, it may be all to the good if the Jerries manage to land here. Lost they'll be, and a good thing, too.'

Laura managed to murmur something non-committal. Not speaking the language herself, she had no idea what the woman was talking about but, like everyone else, she knew about the precautions being taken in case the threatened invasion ever took place. Road signs had been taken down and the Home Guard had been trained to watch for German spies coming in by parachute.

Laura was both disappointed and alarmed by the fact that Neil hadn't put in an appearance at his mother's funeral. His commanding officer had been notified of the death and although she'd heard nothing she'd hoped he would be given compassionate leave to attend. It was months since she'd seen him, and the ache in her heart caused her to blink back angry tears at unexpected moments. If it wasn't for this beastly war, she'd be living an ordinary, uneventful life with him instead of being left to bring up four lively children all on her own.

'Where's Dad?' Mark kept asking as they took their places in the old Norman church. 'You said he'd be here, Mum. Why hasn't he come?'

'Hush, love. I said he'd come if he could. Perhaps he couldn't be spared.'

Mark stuck out his lower lip. 'Then he should have let us know. He should have said!'

Privately Laura agreed with him, but there likely hadn't been time. They weren't on the phone — few ordinary people were — and a letter could have been held up by the censors.

Probably one would be waiting for her when they got back to Hertfordshire.

She felt at peace as they followed the coffin out to the graveyard with its ancient yews and crumbling stones. Small white clouds hung in an azure sky, and birds flew back and forth across the grass. It was a perfect summer day; making it all the harder to believe there was death and destruction happening just across the English Channel.

At last the funeral rites were over and the boys were free to scamper about.

'Where are we going now, Mum?'

'Back to Lilac Lane. The lady next door has invited us in for a cup of tea.'

'I don't like tea, Mum,' Mark pouted. 'Can't we stay outside and play?'

'Well, I suppose so, but don't you get up to any mischief, mind!'

Emily Lucas had lived alone in her

pretty cottage at number four, Lilac Lane, ever since her husband had died some years before. To townbred Laura it seemed to be deep in the country, although it was on the outskirts of the village. The fact that it backed on to a big private estate with what seemed like miles of woods and fields only added to the illusion. Emily's husband, Matt, had been gamekeeper on the estate 'man and boy' as he liked to say. '*Head* keeper,' his wife-would say proudly after he had risen to the height of his profession.

The little Welshwoman who welcomed Laura into number three was short and dark, with her hair twisted into the style known as 'ear phones'. Laura, who wore her hair in a fashionable 'victory roll', noticed that most of the women hereabouts either wore the braided style which Mrs Jenkins had adopted, or had an Eton crop, which didn't suit many people.

'Mrs Lucas will be missed,' the neighbour announced. 'I wonder who we'll get next door now? Somebody quiet, I hope. There's sad it is that your husband couldn't come to his dear mam's funeral! Something to do with the war, I suppose. Whatever next? In the army, is he? Where is he now, then?'

Laura bit her lip. 'I'm not exactly sure. He was sent somewhere for special training, or that's what they said. He wasn't allowed to tell me where.'

Mrs Jenkins nodded. 'Walls have ears! One of those spies, is he? They'll be sending him abroad to find out what Hitler's up to, I daresay.'

'Oh, no, I don't think it's that,' Laura protested, unable to picture her Neil dabbling in secret codes and short-wave radios, but then, she couldn't imagine what he actually was doing, either.

'What about your husband, Mrs Jenkins? Is he in the services?'

'Oh, he's far too old for that sort of thing, but he's in the Home Guard, of course. We have a son in the Royal Air Force, though, training to be a bomber pilot, so one way or another we're all doing our bit. More tea for you, Mrs Lucas? I can wet the pot again if you like. I keep the kettle on the hob all day, see, although it's a proper nuisance having to use the same tea over and over again because of this old rationing!'

They moaned companionably about the trouble involved in eking out the weekly food rations, and in making their clothing coupons last the year.

'It must be hard for you with two little boys to feed and dress, Mrs Lucas.'

'Four!' Laura explained. 'I have two younger ones at home, a little girl and a two-year-old boy. It's not too bad, really. My neighbour's husband came over and dug up our lawn and we've got vegetables planted there. I did grieve over my lovely roses, but there you are! It's all part of the war effort, I suppose.'

★ ★ ★

Laura's two youngest greeted her as if she'd been gone for a month. 'I should go away more often!' She laughed. 'How did they behave, Dot? Didn't give you any trouble, I hope?'

'They were as good as gold. How did you get on at the funeral? Many there, were there?'

Matthew and Mark had rushed off to find their friends and John and Lavinia were sitting under the table, playing with a tin truck and a battered doll. Laura had managed to find some small toys in the village shop in Wales and had promised to hand over these presents at bedtime, provided they played nicely now while she sat down to exchange news with Dorothy.

She had brought over a spoonful of her own tea ration in a twist of greaseproof paper and could enjoy a cup without feeling she was taking advantage of her friend.

'I don't know how to say this, Dot, but it looks as if we'll be moving down to Wales.'

'No! Not after all you said when Neil wanted you to go down there before! Why now? And where will you live?'

'That's the thing, Dot. Gran's cottage will be standing empty now and if I don't do something about it, the council will take it over and who knows who they'll put in there? Strangers who'll chop up the banisters for firewood or keep coal in the bath? That's what the neighbours are afraid of. Anyway, I've decided that we'll move in. It's a quiet sort of place and there's a good school for the children. No rent to pay, either.'

'But it's a tied cottage, surely,' Dorothy protested. 'Didn't it go with your father-in-law's job?'

'Ah, but that's the beauty of it,' Laura explained. 'Neil's father was an ordinary working chap, but he married above him, as the saying goes — not that we ever thought of it like that. Gran's parents were well-to-do farmers and they quite approved of Matt, and they bought the cottage as a wedding present. They got the place for a song because it was a bit tumbledown, but Matt did it up and it's a little jewel now.'

'I'm happy for you, if it's what you want, but I'll miss you, Laura,' Dorothy mused.

'I'll miss you too, but I think I'm doing the right thing, Dot.'

'I'm sure you are. What does Neil think about it all? Is he pleased?'

Laura bit her lip. 'Neil doesn't know. That is, he knows about the cottage belonging to the family, of course, but I haven't been able to get in touch yet to tell him what's been decided. I dashed off a letter to him on the train, but I won't get an answer for a bit. To tell you the truth, I'm getting anxious about why I haven't heard from him. I do hope nothing's happened to him.'

'You'd have heard if it had,' her friend assured her, but she frowned as she said it.

# Alone and Far Away

Without Neil there to help with the packing, the task of moving to Wales seemed almost impossible. Laura had managed to scrounge two tea chests which would hold most of her kitchen equipment and other bits and pieces.

'Just imagine how much tea these must have held in their time,' she marvelled to Dot. 'This whole street's ration for goodness knows how many years!'

'Perhaps you'll be able to grow some sort of herbs down in the country and make a brew from that,' Dot said vaguely. 'I hear some people are roasting acorns or dandelion roots as a coffee substitute.'

'I'll stick with tea, thank you!'

Dot wiped a tear from her eye. 'I'm going to miss you horribly, Laura. We've been friends for so long, it won't be the same without you.'

'You can come down to Wales and visit us,' Laura told her, dabbing at her own eyes with a scrap of pre-war lace handkerchief.

'Of course I will,' Dot sniffed. 'You won't be able to keep me away.'

Privately, each woman was thinking the same thing, that travelling was just too difficult, what with the trains being packed with servicemen and women and never arriving on time because of hold-ups on the line.

'And when this business is over, and we've put Hitler in his place, we'll all have lovely holidays, wearing lovely new clothes and eating fit to burst,' said brave Laura, but it was a pipe-dream and they both knew it.

Suddenly the news from the war was horribly grim. On the 19th of August more than six thousand men took part in a raid on the port of Dieppe in northern France which was then in German hands. The idea was to launch an attack, meant to create havoc among the German defences, and then retreat on the next tide, all within about nine hours.

The attack force, made up mainly of Canadians, supported by British Commandos and other groups, was transported across the English Channel by the Royal Navy under an escort of Royal Air Force Spitfires. The fleet of 252 ships carrying troops and equipment arrived off Dieppe at three o'clock in the morning and these gallant men transferred to their landing craft and prepared to storm the beaches.

Almost at once everything went wrong. The tanks they had brought with them were either destroyed by German machine-gunfire or were hampered by the shingle on the beaches. Men were cut down in droves by enemy fire when they landed on the beaches. The Luftwaffe flew into action against the air and naval forces and thirty-four British ships were sunk and more than a hundred aircraft downed.

The carnage was terrible. Almost a

thousand Canadians were killed and close to two thousand more were taken prisoner. Several hundred British servicemen were killed, including commandos, men of the Royal Navy and the Royal Air Force. In all, more than two thousand men were wounded.

In later years the bloodbath of Dieppe was to be remembered as one of the worst military disasters ever experienced by the Allied forces. For the people of Britain the events of that summer morning came as a terrible shock, although they knew nothing of the strategy behind it. What was Mr Churchill up to? All they could do was hope that 'Winnie' would somehow manage to turn the tide, because it was unthinkable that some day Hitler's forces might come to power in Britain, as they already had in much of Europe.

'Those poor Canadians!' Dorothy mourned as she and Laura chatted over the garden fence two days later. 'Imagine coming all the way from Canada to finish up like this. Some of them were just schoolboys, you know.'

'It's not just them,' Laura mumbled. 'It's all those British commandos as well.'

'Well, I feel sick as mud for them as well, of course,' Dorothy agreed. Then it dawned on her. 'Laura, no! You don't mean Neil?'

'I don't know what to think. He's in the commandos, of course, and as you know they sent him off somewhere on some sort of training course and I haven't heard a thing since. War or no war, you'd think he'd have managed to get in touch after his poor mother died, but he didn't. Now I'm wondering if he was part of this Dieppe thing, or why all the secrecy?'

Her friend struggled to find something useful to say, and failed. The newspapers were full of dreadful news, but as her husband was constantly telling her, they probably didn't dare to print everything, for fear of spreading alarm and despondency. Or, worse, they were forbidden from giving out vital information for spies to pick up on. You had to read between the lines and try to imagine yourself in the shoes of 'them' up in Parliament. What more could there possibly be that the public were not allowed to know?

'Do try not to worry; I expect you'll hear about Neil soon,' Dot said at last.

'That's what I'm afraid of,' Laura murmured.

Her worst fears came true when the dreaded telegram eventually arrived, confirming not only that Neil had been involved in the raid on Dieppe, but was also missing in action.

'Can you come round, Auntie Dot? Mum's had a letter and she's awfully upset.'

Dorothy swung around from the front window to find young Mark Lucas regarding her with a frightened expression. She had seen the telegraph boy stopping at Laura's door and knew it meant only one thing. She had been dithering over whether she should go to her friend at once, or give her some time alone, but now the decision was taken out of her hands.

'Where's Matthew just now?'

'He's out collecting newspapers, Auntie.'

'All right, here's what I want you to do. Take Lavvy and John out to the garden and keep them busy out there until I tell you to come in.'

'But it's spitting rain, Auntie.'

'Then take them upstairs, all right? You must do as I say, Mark, do you understand? This is really important.'

The child nodded solemnly, watching hopefully as she took down a canister from the top shelf which held the last of her sweet ration.

'There are six toffees here,' she explained, pushing them into his hand. 'How many does that make for each of you?'

'Does Matt get some?'

'Not just now. I'll see if I can find something for him later.'

'Then it's two each!' he gloated, and she nodded sadly, looking ahead to the moment when not all the toffees in the world would be of comfort to him.

Laura was pale but calm when Dorothy entered the kitchen, having seen the youngsters settled happily upstairs.

'There's tea in the pot. Help yourself,' Laura said dully. 'He's gone, Dot. Missing in action. That means dead, doesn't it?'

'Certainly not! He could be lying wounded in some hospital somewhere, or hiding where the Germans can't find him. One of these days he'll turn up like a bad penny.'

'Maybe.' Laura sounded listless and unconvinced. 'Oh, why did he have to go and join those wretched commandos? Why couldn't he have stayed in the police force and done his bit here in England? But no! When they came looking for recruits he was the first one with his hand up. I reminded him that he had four kiddies to think of, but all he said was that the thousands of other chaps who'd joined up were husbands and fathers, too, so that wouldn't wash.'

'I remember wondering at the time why they came asking for volunteers from the police,' Dorothy ventured.

'Because commandos have to be able to act on their own initiative, he said,' Laura explained. 'In their line of work they have to make decisions without waiting for orders from some superior officer, and bobbies are used to acting on their own, out on patrol.'

Dorothy brightened as another thought crossed her mind.

'I suppose that means you'll be staying here now, at least until you know for sure what's happened. You need your friends at a time like this.'

Her jaw dropped when Laura said, 'Oh no, Dot! We'll be going ahead with the move as planned. That's what Neil would have wanted.'

No matter how hard Dorothy tried to persuade her, Laura could not be moved.

'Everything's all packed except for the last bits and pieces, and the removal van is coming on Thursday. The children are looking forward to it, and it'll take their minds off what has happened. When I tell them, that is.'

Dorothy was aghast. 'You mean you haven't told them yet?'

'No, I haven't, and you're not to say anything either. Promise me you won't.'

'Well, of course, if that's what you want — but do you think you're doing the right thing? Mark already knows that something's up. Surely you shouldn't keep it from them?'

'Nothing's certain yet, so why get them all upset before we have to? I'll just say that Mummy has had some bad news and leave it at that.'

'Perhaps you're right. But what about you? I hate to think of you down there in Wales trying to keep all this to yourself.'

'I shan't go to pieces if I have work to occupy me, Dot. I'm going to notify the authorities of my new address, but if they send word here, you can forward it to me.'

The sound of childish voices raised in fury floated down from above and Mark thundered down the stairs.

'Mummy! Mummy! John's gone potty on the floor . . .'

'All right, love, I'm coming!' Laura called, before she could be disgraced in front of her friend by further unpleasant revelations. The news from the war might be bleak, but meanwhile there were crises to be attended to on the home front.

\* \* \*

The journey from London to Cardiff was never-ending. The worst part was the frequent, never explained, stops in the middle of nowhere, while the passengers fretted and fumed, longing for the lurching and clanking which would indicate that they were on the move again.

Comics had been read, sweets consumed, and games of I-spy and spot-the-traffic had long since lost their appeal. Laura was thankful when the other two occupants of the compartment left the train at Newport, leaving the Lucases free to sing *Ten Green Bottles* and *She'll Be Coming Round The Mountain* without disturbing others. However, soon that began to pall too, and John started to grizzle. He eventually fell asleep with his thumb in his mouth, and Laura didn't have the heart to pull it out again, despite her strong views on the subject. Anything for peace!

'Well, isn't this nice?' she said brightly, beaming at her three older children with an assurance she was far from feeling. 'Just a few more hours and we'll be settled in our new home. You'll love it there, I know.'

'I loved it where we were.' Mark pouted. 'I don't like leaving all my mates behind.'

'There probably won't be bombs where we're going,' Matthew reminded him, but apparently that was no consolation.

'I know, and I was hoping to see one land on Leicester Road School,' he grumbled. 'I wanted to see it smashed to bits. Boom! Boom!'

'That's not very nice, Mark! Suppose there were people inside?'

'It might have come at night, Mum. Not like that time that the Jerry plane went over you in the garden.'

'Let's not talk about that now. You're going to a nice new school and you won't be long making friends.'

That brought forth a spate of questions.

'Will everybody there speak Welsh? How will we know what they're saying?'

'What *is* Welsh, anyway? Is it like French?'

'Do they play football there?'

'No, they all play the harp,' Laura rejoined, immediately regretting it when she saw their faces. Would she never learn that it didn't pay to be sarcastic with children?

Feeling a tug at her sleeve she looked down to see the anxious face of her only daughter, who clearly had something weighty on her mind.

'Mum? Mum, I don't want to be called Lavinia any more, all right?'

'Whyever not? It's a beautiful name. That was my grandma's name. She died before you were born, but I know she'd have been pleased to have a little baby named after her.'

'It's cos they all call me Lavvy,' the child told her, overcome with shame. 'Annie Menzies said I've got that name cos I'm dirty, and I'm not, am I, Mum?'

Laura's heart went out to her daughter. Children could be so cruel. She gave the girl a quick hug, while thinking fast.

'Well, we're going to have a new home, and a new life, so why not a new name as well? What would you like to be called, then?'

'Mary, or Polly. Not Anne, cos of Annie Menzies. I hate her.'

'You can't have anything too different, can she, Mum?' Ten-year-old Matthew was thinking this through and had put his finger on the difficulty. 'Our names are on our identity cards and ration books. If you call yourself Polly they might not give you anything to eat.'

Laura didn't think it would make much difference but she nodded and pretended to think hard.

'Vinnie, then. Shall we call you that?'

Unfortunately Mark chose that moment to throw one of his giddy fits.

'Vinnie, Vinnie, lost her pinny, then they called her moaning Minnie!' He rolled off the seat, delighted with his own wit.

Tears welled up in his sister's eyes as she looked to her mother for help.

'Viney, then — that would be pretty, like a flower,' Laura said, frowning at Mark and lifting a threatening hand in the direction of his bare leg. His sister laughed happily, and so Viney it was.

★ ★ ★

The cottage at number four, Lilac Lane, met with everyone's approval and the children immediately rushed off to explore. There were three bedrooms tucked under the sloping ceilings and, charming as they were, Laura could foresee some bumped heads before the new occupants learned to sit up carefully when getting out of bed. She gave the largest room to the two boys, saying that she would take John in with her until he got a bit bigger, and then he would have to share with them. Viney was delighted with the tiniest room of all, which had a view across miles of fields.

Longing for a hot drink, Laura stared at the brick fireplace with some trepidation. She wasn't used to cooking with coal, and this had an open grate with a hob on each side, and a small oven in the wall, fronted with an iron door.

She supposed that there was coal in the shed but oh, how she wished for her dear old gas cooker!

'Welcome to Lilac Lane, Mrs Lucas!' The back door had swung open without her noticing it and there stood Mrs Jenkins from next door, an unlikely looking angel in a wrap-around pinny and carpet slippers, with holes cut out to accommodate her bunions. In her hands she carried a tray bearing a large brown teapot and what looked like a loaf of some sort.

'I made *bara brith* this morning,' she announced, as she put the tray down on the table. 'It's not what it should be, mind, when we can't get the proper fruit. Still, I've been keeping a bit by me for a special occasion, so I've done my best.'

*Bara brith* appeared to be a sort of fruit loaf. Laura was greatly touched, and said so.

The older woman beamed. 'We all have to do our bit, don't we? You'll be tired out after coming all that way, I know. And in case you've nothing in for your suppers, there's five eggs in the larder, one for each of you. I keep hens, you see.'

'A whole egg each!' Laura was overwhelmed. And fresh eggs at that, not the horrid powdered stuff.

'Glad to help, I am, but don't go spreading the word, see?' Mrs Jenkins warned. 'The government is that fussy about how many laying hens we can keep, for all we're supposed to be feeding the nation on home produce instead of relying on imported stuff. My son-in-law keeps a few of my hens at their place, see, just in case those inspectors come nosying around. I can't see anything wrong with that, mind you. That old Hitler isn't here yet, so why should some little tin gods try to tell us what we should do with what's our own, when all's said and done?'

Faced with the prospect of cooking five lovely fresh eggs, Laura could only agree.

Later that evening she peeped in at her sleeping children, greatly comforted by the fact that they were all safely under one roof and well fed and healthy. For all their lively independence by day the older boys looked young and defenceless in sleep, while young Viney seemed contented in her little room. Young John was another matter. Tossing and turning on the camp-bed beside Laura's bed, he kept calling out for her, demanding drinks of water.

She understood that he just needed reassurance in this strange new environment, but after she had gone to him for the fifth time and still he failed to settle, she was in danger of losing her temper with him. She was exhausted after the stress of the day and her nerves were all on edge. There was nothing for it but to turn in as well.

Having blown out the candles she stood at the bedroom window, looking out on the moonlit scene. The air was still, and somewhere an owl hooted. How many times had Neil's gaze fallen on these same fields and woods while he listened to the night noises? She caught her breath at the idea.

'Oh, Neil!' she whispered. 'Where are you now?' All across the civilised world, women were feeling the anguish which she was experiencing now, of that she was sure, over fathers, husbands, lovers, sons, killed, maimed or in danger. It was not knowing that was the worst. If it happened that Neil was gone for good she would do her best to bring up his children as he would have wanted. But how could she carry on bravely from day to day if nobody could tell her what had become of him? What if his body was never found or identified?

'Mummy!' came a frightened voice from beside her bed and she turned towards the sound to comfort her youngest child.

'Go to sleep, lovie. Mummy's here.'

# Waifs and Strays

'This is my girl, Gladys.' Mrs Jenkins introduced her daughter with a glow of pride. 'She'll show you around a bit if you like. Make sure you don't get lost.'

'That's very kind.' Laura nodded to the silent Gladys. 'I'll soon have to register at the shop if we want our rations.'

'Not today, it's early closing, but you could go for a walk,' Mrs Jenkins offered. 'You take her up past the Hall, our Glad, and let Mrs Lucas see where her husband's grandfather used to work.'

So they set off down the lane, somewhat hampered because Viney insisted on bringing her doll's pram with her, and John trundled behind on his fairy cycle.

Gladys smiled when Laura apologised for their slow progress. 'It doesn't bother me. Nice to get out when the weather's good. We'll have to save the fairy well for another day, though. We'll never get across the fields with that tricycle.'

'A fairy well!' Viney's ears pricked up at once. 'Will we see fairies, then?'

'Oh, the fairies have gone long ago, that's if there ever were any in the first place.' Gladys turned to Laura to explain. 'It's an old spring, really. Been there since Adam was a boy, I shouldn't wonder. People still use it as a wishing well. You drop in a pin and you get your wish. Wicked superstition, our minister says, but there you are!'

'I must try it some day,' Laura murmured. 'In the meantime, where is this Hall Mrs Jenkins mentioned?'

'Not far now. Mind you, we can't get too close. It's all fenced off with barbed wire these days. The family had to move out when the government took the place over. Some sort of hush-hush thing, with people up from London. Too bad, really. I was parlourmaid up there before I was married, but none of the locals gets a foot inside the door now.'

'But surely the place still has to be cleaned?' Laura objected.

Gladys shrugged. 'They brought their own people with them. My Glyn talks to them in the Red Dragon sometimes, but they don't say much. Signed the Official Secrets Act, he reckons.'

'So your husband isn't in the services, then?'

'Oh no — he's a miner, see? Reserved occupation. Mam was saying that your man got killed at Dieppe. There's sorry we were to hear it.'

'Actually, we don't know that at the moment,' Laura admitted.

'Oh, well, while there's life, there's hope,' Gladys responded, which perhaps was not a tactful way of putting it, but Laura supposed she meant well.

The Hall now came into view, a barracks-like house which seemed to be all windows. If it wasn't for the ivy which covered much of the walls it would have been a stark looking place.

'Those are the stables,' Gladys said, pointing, 'but there's no horses any more. They use them for something, though, cos I've seen men going in and out. Now, this little lane here goes straight to the High Street, so we'll go along there and give you a look at our fair city.' She laughed, as well she might, Laura thought, when she surveyed the two streets which made up the shopping district.

'There's the school you'll be going to next month,' Gladys told the children, 'and over there is the park with the football pitch and all that. There's a bit of a lending library in the back of the newsagent's if you like to read, Mrs Lucas, and the bus comes through once a week if you need to go to the town.'

'Do call me Laura.' It wasn't so much that she wanted to be on first-name terms with Gladys, although she seemed pleasant enough, but she had no idea what her surname was, for Mrs Jenkins had neglected to tell her.

'I think you've seen everything now,' Gladys said, not taking up Laura's invitation, 'so if you don't mind I'll have to be getting home. I expect you can find your own way back?' With that she sauntered off.

Wondering if she'd said something wrong, Laura watched her go, taken aback by the abrupt dismissal. Finally, having mentally reviewed the harmless conversation and reassured herself that it must just be Gladys's way, she turned back in the direction they had come.

This was a small Welsh village, she reminded herself. Of course things were different here from a bustling English town near London. At least people were making an effort to help her settle in, although how much of that was due to the fact that they believed her to be a war widow she couldn't know.

\* \* \*

Laura faced down the official at her door with her arms folded across her apron and a wary look in her eye. He was a pompous little man with a few strands of hair carefully arranged across his balding head, and by the look of his drab suit he was probably an elder in the chapel, or whatever they called them here.

The worst part as far as she was concerned was his speech, which was that of a man who had spoken Welsh all his life and who had only recently, with great reluctance, taken up the English tongue. His grammar was perfect, when she could make out what he was trying to tell her, but his accent was so foreign to her ears that he might as well have been speaking Greek.

'Overflow, you see!'

Laura thought he had something to do with the Water Board.

'The pump is quite all right, thank you,' she told him. Used as she was to taps, she resented having to pump water, but that was life in the country.

'Na, na.' He sounded as exasperated as he looked. 'I'm the billeting officer, see? This house is needed to accommodate new people working at the Hall. They've run out of sleeping space up there and this house is ideal for the purpose. You'll have to move out, I'm afraid.'

'Oh, no, I won't! This is my home now and I'm staying put!'

The little man consulted his clipboard again. 'It says here that the owner died recently. Nothing about squatters moving in without permission.'

'The owner was my mother-in-law, Mrs Lucas. This house is now the property of my husband, so we have every right to be here. He's in the commandos,' she added, hoping to intimidate the official, but apparently that cut no ice with him.

'How many bedrooms?'

'Three.'

'How many people in the house?'

'Five. Myself and my four children.'

'Boys? Girls?'

'Three boys, one girl.'

He made a note of this. 'I think we

can fit two people in, then. The boys can go in one room and the little girl can sleep with you. The lodgers can have her room.'

'But it's tiny!' Laura bleated, but he simply tucked his pencil behind his ear and marched off.

'You'll be hearing from us soon,' he called back over his shoulder.

'What am I going to do?' Laura cried, when she had dashed out to the garden and called across the back fence to Mrs Jenkins. 'I have more than enough to do with four kiddies to take care of, and what if they send me two men? I don't want strange men living in such close quarters with us. It's not decent!'

'Oh, don't you take no notice of that Viv Thomas!' her neighbour declared. 'Him and his clipboard! Thinks he's running the war all by himself, he does! Just tell him to run back to his allotment and attend to his cabbages. That house belongs to you and there's nothing he can do about it.'

That wasn't strictly true, of course.

The people at the Hall had far more clout than their former gamekeeper's daughter-in-law, yet even they had been driven out of the house that had been the family home for centuries and been replaced by government workers. A state of war gave the government extraordinary powers.

Laura said all this to Mrs Jenkins.

'Well, then, girl, the thing to do is fill up your house with evacuees, and then they can't tell you you're not doing your bit. Don't you have any nephews and nieces you can take in?'

'I'm an only child, and Neil's only sister lives in Australia. And if I did have somebody it would have to be a little girl. The boys' room is jam-packed as it is.'

Mrs Jenkins hesitated. 'My cousin in Bettws has had an evacuee from London for quite a while now. Five or six years old, she must be. But it hasn't worked out too well. Blodwen isn't young any more and the girl is too much for her. I had a letter only this morning complaining about the child. She'd like to get rid of her, but the billeting woman says there's nowhere else for her to go, so she has to stay where she is. If the girl could come to you, you'd be doing my poor cousin a real service.'

'I suppose I could think about it,' Laura ventured.

'I'll write to her this very night,' Mrs Jenkins promised. 'Just leave it all to me, and all your troubles will be over.'

Laura thought it might be a case of out of the frying pan into the fire, but how much trouble could one small girl be? And anything was better than being at the beck and call of two demanding adults.

★   ★   ★

Everyone had a story to tell when it came to evacuees. Many thousands of children and quite a few mothers had been sent away from the big cities to avoid the bombing. Ordinary people were expected to play host to these exiled townsfolk and the resulting chaos was a shock all round. Country folk complained about bed-wetting children who arrived covered in lice, while youngsters from decent homes often found themselves thrust into appalling conditions of the sort that their parents had only previously discovered in the pages of Dickens.

Needless to say there were numerous cases where children thrived under the care of kindly foster parents, forging affectionate relationships which continued throughout their lives, but those were not remarked on by the Press.

Even so, the new arrivals often found it hard to adjust to what they found in the country. To think that milk came from cows instead of starting out in a nice, clean bottle! What was the world coming to?

'What's wrong with the little girl your cousin took in?' Laura asked Mrs Jenkins. 'I mean, does she steal or something?' The Lucas children might be no angels, but there was no vice in them, and Laura didn't relish the thought of letting some infant Fagin or Artful Dodger loose among them.

'She tells lies!' Mrs Jenkins said with awful relish. 'Absolute whoppers, she tells, and our Blodwen can't abide with that, her being such a staunch Methodist.'

'I see. Perhaps she does it out of fear of being punished or something.'

'Oh, it's not like that, Mrs Lucas. She comes out with the wildest tales, things no sensible person would believe for a minute, and no reason for it at all.'

Laura thought she understood. Torn away from her family and everything she knew, the child probably invented a fantasy life to help her cope. Perhaps there was an imaginary friend, or an unshakeable belief that her mother would turn up at any moment to make everything all right again.

When the news was broken to her family, they reacted in various ways. Matthew merely grunted. Always a keen Cub, he had recently gone up to Scouts and was now attempting to pass the Tenderfoot Test. If only he could get the hang of that wretched sheepshank he would sail through it.

All over Britain the Scouts were performing sterling service for the war effort, and it wasn't just a case of collecting newspapers, as he'd done up to now. Scouts were even performing acts of valour, such as rescuing people from bombed buildings or assisting with fire-watching. Matthew longed to be like them.

Mark scowled. 'Do we have to have her, Mum? It means there'll be less food for all of us.'

Rationing was a real nuisance, and it was coming to something when you could feel like cheering after queuing for hours and coming home triumphantly with half a pound of sausages, as she herself had done this morning. And such sausages! Nobody quite knew what went into them.

'She'll have her own ration book,

Mark. You won't go short,' she assured him, but he scowled again, unconvinced.

It was Viney who would be most affected, since she would have to share her room with a stranger.

'I think I'm going to hide Rosebud,' the child said solemnly, 'in case that girl breaks her.' Rosebud was a grubby rag doll which Viney had kept since babyhood. She was really too old for it now, but it represented security to her.

The little girl was to come in on the bus on Thursday morning, and Laura walked up to the bus stop with Viney holding one hand and John the other.

The bus was late, but at last it chugged to a halt, disgorging women loaded down with bulky packages and untidy string bags. You were told it was unpatriotic to hoard, but for most people the motto was 'grab it while you can get it' because you never knew when you were going to see another one of whatever it was you couldn't do without.

The child was the last one off the bus and Laura's heart went out to the poor mite. Taller than Viney, but very thin, she was dressed in someone's cast-off skirt that was too long for her and a bedraggled macintosh that was too short in the sleeves. Her straight flaxen hair looked as if it needed a good wash, and her woebegone little face was covered in smuts. She carried a grubby pillowcase which apparently held all her worldly goods.

Laura stepped forward to take the poor little waif into her arms and was amazed when the child drew herself up and held out a polite hand.

'Are you Mrs Lucas? I am the Lady Sybilla!'

Viney's hand went to her mouth to stifle a giggle, and John's jaw dropped.

'Two can play at that game.' Laura grinned and inclined her head graciously, saying, 'And I am the Duchess of Carmarthen! How do you do?'

'Mum said a fib,' John whispered.

'I think they're playing a game,' Viney

whispered back. 'Mum told me her name's Sybil Waite.'

Sybil obediently followed them home, all the wind taken out of her sails by Laura's response. She was used to outraged gasps, even a sharp slap on the bare leg, but this was something new. This Mrs Lucas seemed nothing like Auntie Blodwen, as she had been made to call her previous foster parent.

When they turned into the tree-lined way leading to Lilac Lane she caught a glimpse of the Hall and her eyes opened wide.

'Is that where you live? Is your mum a real duchess, then?' she asked Viney. 'I thought she was just pretending.'

'She was, cos you said you're the Lady Sybilla, but you're not, are you?'

'Sometimes I am, when I'm being rescued by Robin Hood or someone. What's your name, then?'

'It's Viney.'

'Funny name that. I never heard it

before. So, is that your house over here?'

'Of course it's not my house, silly! We live in Lilac Lane, and if you don't like it you can lump it, so there!'

For some reason this struck them both as being highly amusing, and they ran ahead of Laura, laughing like maniacs. She watched them go with some relief. If they were going to be friends it would make things much easier for them all.

Viney was a shy child, slow to make friends. Laura had been afraid of what might happen to her when she started at the village school in September, especially as all the children round about seemed to speak Welsh. Viney would be regarded as a little foreigner, and might be isolated. The boys would attend the same school, of course, but Llanidris was an old-fashioned place where the boys and girls had separate playgrounds.

Now there was Sybil, and that would be a great help. Even so, Laura could have had no idea that this partnership was something which would last throughout their lives, giving them strength when they needed it most.

# Yet Another Mouth To Feed!

September. School was in session and all four children had gone, more or less willingly, to school. The house was quiet and Laura relished the silence. One way or another it had been a hectic summer and she was glad to have time to herself at last.

It was a perfect autumn day. The sun was shining and the leaves had not yet begun to fall. The hedgerows were heavy with fruit of all kinds, and Laura wondered if she should make one more blackberry-picking expedition. She didn't have enough sugar to make bramble jelly but, combined with apples from their own small orchard, the berries could be made into a pudding.

On the other hand there was a pile of sewing to do. The hem needed letting down on Viney's Sunday frock, and something had to be done about the ugly hand-me-downs that poor Sybil wore. There might be a war on, but that was no excuse for letting her go about looking like a tinker's child.

The letter-box rattled and Laura took her time about going to see what the postman had brought. Nothing but bills, probably, unless there was a letter from Dot. She always looked forward to Dot's letters, even though they contained nothing that Laura didn't already know; comments on the restrictions brought about by the war, usually. The National Loaf tasted horrible, eggs were scarce, and Dot hadn't seen a decent cut of meat for weeks.

Laura's heart missed a beat when she saw the envelope that was lying in solitary state on the doormat. It was what she had been both longing for and dreading, the letter which would give her news of her husband's fate.

She turned it over in her hand and then thrust it into her apron pocket.

She wouldn't read it yet. If he was dead, she wanted to put off the awful finality of the news as long as possible. As long as she didn't look at the grim words, set down in black and white, he would still be alive, or so she believed.

★　★　★

The loud rapping continued and at last Laura was forced to get up and answer the door.

'I'm sorry, Mrs Jenkins, I was just . . . ' Her voice trailed off.

'I don't mean to intrude, Mrs Lucas, but Evans the Post told me. 'She's had one of them nasty letters,' he says, 'and most of the time they're bad news. So you better get round there quick, *bach*, just in case.' So here I am, Mrs Lucas, not wanting to be nosy, see, only extending the hand of friendship if it's needed.'

'You're very kind, Mrs Jenkins. I don't know what to say.'

'You can start by telling me what's in

that letter. Then if need be we can have a good cry before the kiddies come in from school. Where's young John, by the way? Upstairs sleeping, is he?'

'I haven't opened it yet,' Laura confessed, leading the way into the kitchen.

'Putting it off won't change anything,' Mrs Jenkins said stoutly, although her face was almost as pale as Laura's. 'Give it here, then, and let me see what it says.'

After a moment's hesitation Laura passed over the envelope and waited, trembling, while Mrs Jenkins slit it open with the butter knife and slowly took in the contents.

'It's all right, Mrs Lucas!' she shouted. 'He's alive!'

'Alive? Let me see that!' Laura cried and snatched the letter from her friend.

'It says he's a prisoner of war,' Mrs Jenkins went on, as if Laura couldn't read for herself. 'That's good, isn't it? Leastways it's too bad if them Germans have got hold of him, but at least he's alive, and he must be all in one piece or they'd have said.'

Tears were pouring down Laura's face as a multitude of thoughts raced through her mind.

She didn't like the idea of Neil being in enemy hands, but on the other hand it meant that he wasn't seeing action now, which meant he had a good chance of coming through the war unscathed. Unless he tried to escape, of course.

\* \* \*

'Can I get down, Mum? I want to listen to Children's Hour.' That was Mark, stuffing the remains of his tea into his mouth and already wriggling off his chair.

'No, not yet, Mark. I've something to tell you all. I've had some news.'

'Me too, Auntie?' Sybil sensed that something important was happening.

'Yes, dear. This affects us all.'

'It's about Dad, isn't it?' Matthew guessed.

'Yes, it is. He's alive and well; that's the good news. The bad news is, he's been captured by the enemy and he'll have to stay in one of their prison camps for the time being.'

Viney started to cry. 'What will they do to him, Mum? Are they going to hurt him?'

'No, no,' Laura assured her, although the very same fear was nagging at her mind. 'I expect he'll be living with a lot of other brave men, having a high old time playing football together, or reading books. Perhaps he'll be able to send us letters, telling us all about it.'

'I wish I was old enough to go and fight!' Matthew announced. 'I'd go and give those Germans what-for!'

'I know you would, love.' Laura smiled affectionately at her fierce little son. He looked as if he'd been pulled through a hedge backwards. His shorts, bought too large to allow for growth, sagged below his bony knees, and he had lost his garters, which caused his socks to wrinkle down to his ankles.

Meanwhile, Mark had disappeared and Laura felt a twinge of irritation. Other than saying 'Oh' when he heard the news he had shown no emotion whatsoever.

Viney was crying, Sybil was chewing her fingernails, and John was too young to understand, but Mark hardly seemed bothered. Perhaps he hadn't taken it in properly. She sighed. She would have to keep an eye on him in case he was upset and afraid to let it show.

From that day on the children's games took a different turn. The Lady Sybilla was no longer the fair maiden, waiting patiently to be rescued by her faithful swains. She galloped through the fields with Mark and Viney, searching for prisoners to set free. On the other hand, Matthew seemed to have grown up overnight. All his spare time was spent going out and about with the Scouts, doing useful war work.

He couldn't wait until he was old

enough to take part in fire-watch activities as many were already doing. Not that this would ever be necessary in Llanidris, his mother hoped, for unlike the poor souls in the big cities who were suffering in the Blitz, this little Welsh community was safe from the bombs. For the moment, at least.

Laura had just begun to feel safe from officialdom, now that she had taken Sybil into the house, leaving no room to have any more people billeted on her, when a woman in khaki uniform turned up on the doorstep one afternoon.

'Are you from the Red Cross?' Laura asked the moment she opened the door, thinking this might have something to do with Neil.

'The Red Cross? Me? No, I'm Daisy Waite. Sybil's mother.' She frowned when this elicited no response. 'I am right in thinking that you have my little girl staying with you?'

Laura swiftly recovered from her surprise to exclaim, 'Mrs Waite! Yes, of course. Do come in. Sybil isn't here right now, though; she's at school, along with my lot.'

'How many children do you have, Mrs Lucas? It is Mrs Lucas, isn't it?' Daisy said as she followed Laura through to the kitchen.

'Laura, please. I've four children, including John here.'

The toddler looked up, bestowing a jammy smile on the visitor.

'What a little love! I'd like to have more children when all this is over, although my husband's in the navy so it doesn't do to look too far ahead.'

In return Laura found herself telling her about Neil.

'So I suppose we all have something to worry about these days. I hope you can stay for tea,' she went on brightly. 'Sybil will be so thrilled to see you. Or failing that, you must drop in at the school. You can't leave without seeing her at least for a few minutes.'

'I think I can manage that, if you can spare the food, thanks. I hitched a ride with an army lorry that was passing this way and they've promised to collect me on the way back.

'I can't tell you how relieved I am to know that Sybil has found a nice family here. She wrote to me, you know, poor little love, saying how unhappy she was at her last place, and begging me to come and get her. Can you believe they didn't even let me know she'd left there? Luckily somebody was at home when I called, or I wouldn't have known where to find her.'

'I gathered they were a bit strict,' Laura agreed. 'She's better off here. My little girl Viney is the same age and they've taken to each other quite well. But how did you come to send the child down to Wales? Was it because you were called up?'

'Not exactly. I had to register, of course, like everyone else, but I don't think they'd have forced me to go when I had a young child at home. No, we lived in London, and John and I — that's my husband — thought it might be best if we sent her to my sister in Canada for the duration. She was meant to leave almost two years ago now; we had her passage booked and everything, and then at the last minute she came down with chickenpox and wasn't able to sail. But it was a blessing, for she was meant to be travelling on the *City of Benares*.'

Laura's hand flew to her throat. 'Oh, no! That was the ship that was torpedoed, wasn't it?'

Daisy nodded, her face grim. 'Even now, I can hardly bear to think about it. So many little ones lost, and those that survived spent hours clinging to the lifeboats before being rescued. John knows what it's like to be in the North Atlantic in bad weather, and after that he put his foot down and said that Sybil was staying here.'

'So you decided to have her evacuated so you could join up and do your bit. Well, you can set your mind at rest now, Daisy. I'll do my very best for the child, you can count on that.'

Both women blinked back tears and Daisy enveloped Laura in a warm hug.

At that moment the door burst open and the room filled with children, laughing and shouting.

'Mum! Oh, Mum! I can't believe it's you!' Sybil flew into her mother's arms, a look of joy on her face.

'Upstairs, you lot, and wash your face and hands,' Laura directed, past the lump of emotion in her throat. 'Why don't you take Mummy out and show her the garden, Sybil?'

The pair wandered outside. It was a happy little oasis in the grim desert of war.

★ ★ ★

Finally, one glorious day Laura received a letter from her husband, the first she'd heard from him since the disaster at Dieppe. Not that it said much, being nothing more than a printed paper where the sender could choose from a variety of sentiments, ticking off the ones which applied, such as 'I am well.' Still, it was better than nothing.

She now knew that she could write to Neil in return, sending her letters via the Red Cross in the hope that he would receive them. She knew that the men in the prison camps would treasure such missives from home, but deciding what to put in such a letter was something else again. There was no point in mentioning any news of the war, or what precautions were being taken locally against the feared invasion. Anything like that would be censored and the letter would be a mass of blacked-out remarks.

News of the children was innocuous enough, and would probably be eagerly received by their father, but Laura was careful not to dwell on any problems, or he would be frustrated at being unable to help.

Mark was beginning to be one of those problems. By now he should have been developing a sense of responsibility, like his older brother, and have some thought for others, but this was sadly lacking and she didn't know what to do about it. Growing boys needed a father, yet thousands of children were growing up in one-parent homes because their fathers were away at the war, or had been killed, and so the onus was on their mothers to act the part of both parents. Laura wasn't sure she could cope.

With six people in the house, she decided that the children had to pull their weight, all except John, who was too young. This meant helping in the garden, making their own beds, and helping with the washing-up. However, while the others tackled these tasks with varying degrees of enthusiasm, Mark was openly defiant.

When a plate went crashing to the floor while he and Sybil were doing the dishes one evening, Laura gathered the pieces together impatiently.

'Do be careful, Mark! That's the second one you've dropped this week!

I'll have to see if I can glue this back together.'

As she straightened up from picking up the two pieces she caught sight of a smirk on her son's face. Sybil noticed it as well.

'He does it on purpose, Auntie,' she observed, when Mark had gone off to the room he shared with his brother. 'I heard him telling Matthew that you'd let him off if you thought he was too clumsy.'

'Did he now?' Laura answered grimly. 'That's very interesting — but you know what I've told you about telling tales, Sybil.'

Now what? Laura thought. She couldn't let him get away with that. It wasn't just a case of insisting he do his share of the work, but a moral question as well.

She solved the problem by telling him that his pocket money would be withheld every time he broke something. Not that this would help the china situation. With nothing in the shops you couldn't buy plates for love nor money, unless you were lucky enough to find some in a second-hand shop, a luxury Llanidris didn't have.

The incident of the cheese was far more serious. Food rationing was now quite severe, and one person's cheese ration for the week was a mere two ounces. Laura longed for the days when she'd been able to make lovely macaroni cheese or cauliflower cheese with a crisp golden topping. Her mouth watered at the thought.

'Here's what I've decided,' she explained to her assembled children. 'I'm going to wrap your individual rations in greaseproof paper, with your names on, and keep it on the marble slab in the larder. You can choose whether to eat it early in the week, or save it until later for a treat.'

They liked this idea, which gave them some control over the situation. In a world where no child ever saw an orange or a banana, where ice cream was unavailable and where sweets and chocolate were strictly rationed, treats were few and far between.

All went well until halfway through the first week, when there was an outcry from the larder.

'Mum! My cheese has gone!' This was from Matthew.

'Are you sure you didn't have it earlier, love?'

'No, I was saving it, like you said.'

'And there's a big bite out of mine,' Viney wailed.

'Don't tell me we've got mice!' Laura groaned, drying her hands on her apron and going to see for herself.

'Two-legged mice!' she declared a moment later.

'What do you mean, Auntie?' asked Sybil.

'Well, if mice had been here we'd find bits of chewed paper strewn about, but this has been unwrapped and put back together again. John, did you do this?'

The child shook his head, surveying her anxiously over the thumb that was plugged into his mouth.

'No, you couldn't have reached that high, could you? And you three, you swear it wasn't you?'

Three heads shook, three faces assumed self-righteous expressions.

'Mark!' she bawled.

Mark came slowly downstairs, trying to look unconcerned.

'You've taken something which didn't belong to you, haven't you?' his mother accused him at once.

'No, I never.'

Laura shook her head in dismay. 'Telling fibs just makes matters worse. I've explained what rationing means, Mark. We'd all like to have more, but we can't, so this way at least everyone gets their fair share of what's available. Now, why did you do this?'

He looked up at her, his face the picture of innocence. 'It was just sitting there, and I wanted it.'

'Then I want you to promise never to do anything like this again, and you're to tell Matthew and Viney you're sorry.'

'Sorry,' he muttered, with a distinct

lack of enthusiasm.

'And you promise?'

As he pressed his lips together, refusing to look her in the eye, her temper boiled over and she delivered a series of stinging slaps to his bare leg. He ran out of the room, howling, leaving her feeling guilty and defeated.

'And quite right, too,' Mrs Jenkins said later when Laura confided in her. 'What that boy needs is a good smacked bottom, and if he was mine he'd get it, too.'

'I've always believed it was better to rule by example,' Laura murmured, 'but I find myself letting fly regularly these days. When I went up last night to tuck them in, Mark looked like a little angel lying there asleep. I must admit I shed a few tears as I watched him.'

'Jack the Ripper's mother probably felt the same when he was a boy,' Mrs J. retorted. 'Now don't you give it another thought. We're all a bit on edge these days, and children have to learn.'

Motherhood wasn't all thorns, of course. Laura particularly enjoyed watching her little girls grow in stature and wisdom, for she now thought of Sybil as one of her own, and she was grateful that Viney and the little Londoner got on so well together.

'Who are you going to marry when you grow up?' she heard Sybil ask when the girls were having a dolls' tea-party in the back garden one day.

'How do I know? He hasn't asked me yet,' came Viney's reply.

'I shall marry a lord,' Sybil said, with great confidence. 'Then I really can be the Lady Sybilla for ever and ever.'

Laura smiled to herself. She supposed that there were women who decided what — and who — they wanted and went after it, but for most people it came down to a matter of falling in love, and wanting to be with that person always.

She had chosen Neil for himself and the qualities she had seen in him, and it didn't matter that they would never be rich. She vowed that if only she could get Neil back home, sound in wind and limb, she would never ask for another thing. But that happy day was unlikely to come for some time.

The war ground on. Somehow Hitler's forces were prevented from invading Britain. More and more men from across the British Empire — Canada, Australia, New Zealand, India — joined the fight, and finally the mighty United States of America came out in support of the Allied cause, sending thousands of their own young men to 'do or die'.

In 1944 the D-Day landings in Normandy took place and from then on the writing was on the wall as the Allies fought their way through Europe. Each evening Laura turned on the nine o'clock news and everyone crowded round to hear the sombre voice of the announcer saying, 'This is the BBC Home Service.' Sometimes the news was good, sometimes it was bad, but she reckoned it was better to know what was going on than to remain in ignorance.

And then, just when she thought better days might be on the horizon, Laura found herself fighting a little battle of her own.

It began one day when she opened the door to accept a package from Evans the Post. Sybil's birthday wasn't far off and she had been expecting a present from her mother.

'There's high jinks up at the vicarage,' Evans noted, bright-eyed.

'Has the vicar run off with the organist, then?' she joked and he chuckled. Miss Williams was eighty if she was a day and the vicar not many years her junior.

'It's his wife, *bach*. Been taken bad, see, and off to hospital. Vicar wanted me to bring you the news.'

Laura wondered why. Apart from the fact that it had nothing to do with her, she was well aware that Gwyn Evans needed no prompting to spread the word. He looked on having a good gossip as one of the perks of the job and wasn't above sharing the contents of postcards with all and sundry.

'It's that Ribena that's the trouble, Mrs Lucas.'

Laura was taken aback. The delicious blackcurrant drink had recently been developed with the idea of helping people to get enough Vitamin C now that oranges were no longer available. Had Mrs Smart had some sort of attack after queuing for hours, only to be told on reaching the front of the line that the woman in front of her had pounced triumphantly on the very last bottle? Such things were apt to bring on a fit of hysteria, if nothing else.

'Ribena, Mr Evans?'

'You know, that evacuee girl from up London, her with the baby.'

'Oh, Reubena! What about her?'

'Well, she can't stay there with the vicar, with Mrs Smart gone. Wouldn't be decent. It might be different if her husband came and stayed in the house as well, but between you, me and the gatepost, I don't think there's any such animal.'

'She wears a wedding ring,' Laura murmured.

'Huh! Any fool can slip a ring on her finger without it being the real thing. It's a curtain ring from Woolworth's, if you ask me.'

'I agree it poses a problem — but I don't know what I can do about it . . . ' Her nose told her that the pot she had left on the stove had come to a boil and she had to break off to dash back to the kitchen to prevent a mess.

Evans the Post was still standing on the doorstep when she returned.

'Vicar wants you to come and get them, Mrs Lucas.'

'Me?' She squeaked. 'Surely he knows I've got a full house already?'

'You're Church,' he stated, turning to go, leaving her fuming.

On arriving in Llanidris Laura had soon learned that the first question anyone asked her was, 'How do you like Wales?' and the second was, 'Are you

Church or Chapel?' Translated, this meant you were either Church of England, a rare breed in this part of the world, or Methodist. And it was because she was one of the few adherents to Mr Smart's brand of religion that she had been asked to come to the rescue. Presumably he didn't wish to ask any favours of 'the other side', although there was no conflict between the members, apart from the feeling of superiority each felt towards the unenlightened.

'Come on, John,' she said, buttoning her son into his little blue coat. 'We'd better go and see what's going on. Stand there and don't move while I go and turn off the cooker, and we'll be off.'

He grinned happily, hoping that this meant a stop at the village shop, where, if he was lucky, he would be handed a biscuit for being 'such a pet.'

*　*　*

Reubena Porter was an unattractive girl, pasty-faced and lumpish. When she heaved herself up off the settee and yanked the vicarage door open she was clutching a film magazine in one hand and had a half-smoked cigarette protruding from her lips.

'Yes?'

'I'm Mrs Lucas. I understand that Mrs Smart has been taken to hospital.'

'Yeah.'

'So I've come to invite you to stay with us. It'll be a bit of a squeeze, mind, but just until we see how things are with the Smarts.'

'Why?'

Faced with such blank non-comprehension Laura hardly knew what to say, but she stammered through some sort of explanation, half hoping to meet with a flat refusal.

The girl shrugged. 'OK then. Wait there while I fetch Sidney. I can get the rest of my stuff later.'

Sidney Porter might have been an attractive baby if he hadn't smelled so dreadful. His little face was so streaked with tears that he must have been appealing for help for quite some time before he'd fallen asleep from sheer exhaustion. Laura's hands itched to get the child into a nice warm bath.

'You'd better change him before we go,' she pointed out rather sharply, 'and he'll need more nappies. And doesn't he have a bottle or something?'

Reubena flounced off, performing these motherly tasks as though at the whim of someone who asked too much.

'I gave him a bath last week,' Reubena complained when they were back in Lilac Lane and Sidney was splashing happily in the kitchen sink. 'Too many baths isn't good for a kiddie. Leaves them with their pores hanging open, my mum says, so germs can flood in.'

Laura ignored this gem of wisdom and when Sidney, patted dry and powdered, was tucked up in a dresser drawer, she turned her attention to the problem of sleeping accommodation for his mother.

There was no help for it; she would have to make up a bed on the settee for the time being. Then, as soon as possible, she would go to see the vicar.

She realised that the proprieties had to be observed, but there were spare bedrooms galore in the vicarage. If poor Mrs Smart was kept in hospital, then a chaperone would have to be found. Reubena must have made friends in the village; some other girl could be recruited for the job of evacuee-sitting.

'I'd best be getting back up to the vicarage for my clothes then,' Reubena said, lighting up another cigarette. Apparently it didn't occur to her to say thank you to Laura for putting herself out, or for looking after Sidney.

'You do that,' Laura muttered. She could feel a headache coming on.

The children, when they came home from school, were full of questions. Viney and Sybil were delighted with Sidney.

'Where's his pram, Mum? Can we take him out for a walk?'

'I don't think he has one, Viney. I don't know how long he'll be here, but if he has to stay for a while we'll have to see if we can borrow one. Then you can take him out, if his mum approves.'

There were few prams in Llanidris, not because of the war but because it was the custom for the local women to carry their infants inside the huge shawls they wore. These blanket-like garments were draped over one shoulder and under the opposite arm, with the baby cradled in the folds.

'Why do we have to have him here?' Mark demanded. 'I don't want a howling baby keeping us awake all night.'

'All babies cry,' Laura told him, 'and we'll just have to make the best of it.'

Much to Laura's annoyance, Reubena didn't return. Tea-time came and went with no sign of her. Getting Sybil and Viney ready for choir practice and making sure that the boys did their homework left Laura with little time to worry, and then there was all the fuss of putting up the blackout and making sure that no chink of light showed outside.

When the door flew open at eight o'clock she was all ready to give the girl a piece of her mind, but it was only her own children, coming back from the church hall. Viney was crying softly.

'What's the matter? What happened? Was it those Hughes boys bullying you again?'

'She walked into a lamp-post,' Sybil announced.

'Not again, Viney! Why can't you watch where you're going?'

'How am I supposed to see when the lights are so dim or not on at all?' she sniffed.

'I s'pose that's why people keep telling us to look at the North Star,' Sybil said. 'So we don't go the wrong way and get lost.'

Laura frowned. 'I don't know what you mean, Sybil. Aren't you a bit mixed up?'

'No, Auntie, honestly. That's what people say all the time. North Star!'

Matthew began to laugh. 'Not North Star, silly! *Nos da!* It's Welsh for good night.'

Sybil turned beetroot red and shuffled her feet. 'Well, how was I s'posed to know?'

Mark began to hoot with unkind laughter and Laura had to step in before there was a full-scale squabble.

Busy with the bedtime ritual of snacks and stories, and ignoring pleas for drinks of water, it was past nine before the household was settled and she could turn her attention to what was left of the news. As soon as that was over she would have to prepare a bottle for Sidney — but where was his mother?

★ ★ ★

When Reubena hadn't returned by ten o'clock the following morning Laura marched up to the vicarage to give the girl a piece of her mind. This expedition was achieved with some difficulty; there was no place for the baby in John's pushchair so she had to carry him on one hip while pushing the pram with one hand so that by the time she arrived she was hot and out of breath.

'Mrs Lucas!' The vicar greeted her with surprise. 'You seem to have your hands full there. Where's Mrs Porter?'

'That's what I've come to ask you,' Laura retorted, putting Sidney on the floor. 'Isn't she here? She's been gone all night!'

'Dear me!' The vicar blinked at her through his thick glasses. 'I heard that you'd taken her in, but, of course, she couldn't stay here. My wife . . . '

'Then if she isn't here, where is she? She can't just dump her child on me while she wanders off goodness knows where. Does she have friends in the village, perhaps someone she might

85

have gone to visit?'

The vicar spread his hands helplessly. 'Betty might know, I suppose.'

Betty Parsons was a plump mother of six who earned a few shillings by coming in to clean the vicarage twice a week. When called upon she was obviously bursting to tell what she knew.

'She's gone,' she sniffed. 'Taken all her clothes and make-up. We won't be seeing her again, you can bank on that.'

'Gone?' Laura squeaked. 'But she hasn't taken Sidney! What on earth are we going to do?'

The vicar looked perplexed. 'I don't see what we *can* do. As far as I know the girl is over twenty-one so she has a right to come and go as she pleases — and that's what the police would tell us if we went to them.'

'Perhaps something's happened to her,' Betty suggested, wide-eyed with excitement.

'Something *will* happen to her all right when I catch up with her!' Laura snapped. 'Landing me with her infant without so much as a by your leave! And don't tell me there's a war on!' she told the vicar, who was about to say something placatory. 'Everybody uses that as an excuse for shabby behaviour and it's just not good enough.'

'I quite agree, Mrs Lucas. But in the meantime, this child cannot be left unattended. Perhaps Mrs Parsons . . . '

'Don't look at me, Vicar! I've got my hands full with six at home.'

'So have I!' Laura cried, but she knew she was fighting a losing battle. If possession was nine-tenths of the law then she was — literally — left holding the baby.

★   ★   ★

When a week had passed with no sign of the young mother, Laura realised that she was probably stuck with Sidney, although she chided herself for thinking that way about an innocent baby.

'I'm sure she must be lying dead somewhere,' she told Mrs Jenkins. 'She may have gone up to London and got caught in an air-raid or something.'

'Or she may have met up with some chap and gone off with him,' Mrs Jenkins suggested darkly. 'Always had my suspicions about that girl, I have. Take it from me, she's no good.'

'That's all very well, but what about Sidney?'

'He's hardly your responsibility, Mrs Lucas. He'll have to go to an orphanage. Get the vicar to arrange it. That's what he's there for, to help people out of muddles.'

But Laura couldn't bear the thought of sending poor Sidney to an institution. Such places must be filled to overflowing already with children who had been left orphaned by the Blitz. And she already had to dance attention on five youngsters, so what was one more?

So Sidney stayed, and in time it was as if he had always been there. John grew bigger, and refused to use either the pushchair or his cot; he moved into his brothers' bedroom and Sidney took his place. Sybil and Viney trundled him around the lanes in the aging pram and life settle back into a familiar routine.

So busy was Laura with all the demands of family life that she failed to notice what was happening with Mark. True, he had become more resentful and unhelpful, but she expected him to grow out of that in time. She could sympathise with him when he complained about having to share a bedroom and having no place to keep his treasures, and although she scolded him for giving John a hard slap when the child broke a piece off his beloved train engine she understood his frustration.

So she was totally unprepared when she went into the village shop, ration books in hand, to collect their meagre allowance of food for the coming week, and the grocer said, 'There's sorry I am, Mrs Lucas, but I need a word.'

Nobody else was in the shop and she was taken aback when he strode over to the door and locked it, turning the card over so that it read 'Closed'. She glanced at her wrist-watch, wondering if it had stopped. It was nowhere near lunch-time.

'Yes, Mr Lloyd?'

'It's that boy of yours, young Mark. I don't like to say anything, but theft is theft, after all, Mrs Lucas.'

'Theft!' Laura felt herself go pale.

'I'm afraid so. I've had my eye on him for a bit now. I'm always on the lookout for children loitering too long in one place, so when I caught him at it there was no mistake, see.'

'What did he . . . take, Mr Lloyd?' She couldn't see how it could be sweets. The toffees and pear drops and suchlike were kept in stoppered glass jars, waiting to be weighed out on the brass scales for eager customers claiming their ration of a tiny bag a week.

'Raspberry jam, Mrs Lucas. He took it down off the shelf, bold as brass, and put it under his pullover. I was tempted to give him a thick ear, but thought it best to have a word with you first. There may be some excuse, of course. The boy is new to Llanidris, and doesn't know our ways.'

Laura went home overcome with humiliation. She had paid for the stolen goods and had handed over precious 'points' as well, which meant no jam for tea at all that week. It was a well-known fact that wartime raspberry jam wasn't the real thing anyway, being partly made from parsnips. Some people said that the pips were actually made from wood. Still, it was better than nothing, and now the children were going to be deprived, and all because of Mark.

That wasn't the real issue, of course. As the grocer had said, theft was theft. Her mind flew ahead to the future. She could foresee trouble if this wasn't nipped in the bud, but how to deal with it?

It was lucky for Mark that the girls arrived home from school before he did, as he had gone, by prior arrangement, to play football in the park.

'Mum! Sybil wants to ask you something,' Viney said, nudging her friend.

'We were wondering,' Sybil began hesitantly, 'if we could go to the Welsh Lion on Sunday, Auntie, to listen to the speeches.'

'No, of course you can't,' Laura replied. 'The very idea!'

The two girls exchanged glances. 'I told you she'd say no,' Viney muttered. 'It's because we're Church of England, I suppose.'

It took Laura some time to unravel this puzzle. The local pub was the Red Dragon, not the Lion, and in any case, it wasn't open on Sundays. Drink wasn't sold in Wales on the Lord's Day. And what were these speeches? Intrigued, she mentioned it to Mrs Jenkins the next time they met over the garden fence, and her neighbour gave a hoot of laughter.

'She must mean the Wesleyan, Mrs

Lucas, the Methodist church! Welsh Lion — Wesleyan — see? We've got guest preachers all this month, and their sermons are fair bringing in the crowds. Talk about hellfire and brimstone! You send your little girls along, and they'll come to no harm, although I doubt they'll understand a word that's spoken, as it's all in Welsh!'

Laura thought it too bad that the sermons weren't to be in English. Young Mark could have done with a good dose of that. Instead, she had to decide between stopping his pocket money for a time, or sending him to bed right after tea for a week. Somehow he had to be made to keep to the straight and narrow.

Once again she longed for Neil to come home and resume his place as head of the family. It was all becoming too much for her to cope with.

# Peace At Last

May 1945. The war had ended at last. At least, the conflict in Europe had come to a close, with Germany and Italy defeated. The war against Japan was still in full swing, but people hoped that it was only a matter of time before that ended, too. Meanwhile, there was much to celebrate.

Hearing the bells of All Saints church ringing for the first time since they had come to Llanidris brought tears to Laura's eyes. All church bells had been silent since the beginning of the war, the idea being that they could then be rung to warn people if an invasion began. In the past six years brides had had to do without the joyous clamour of bells as they emerged from the church after their weddings, and the age-old practice of announcing the age of a recently-deceased parishioner by the tolling of a funeral bell had likewise been prohibited. Now the traditions so dear to the hearts of the British people could be gladly taken up again.

'When will Dad be coming home?' Matthew wanted to know.

'Soon now, I hope, love. He's out of the prison camp and on his way back but he'll have to wait to be demobbed. These things take time.'

'What's mobbed?' Viney wondered fearfully. It didn't sound very nice and she had visions of her father having to fight his way through hordes of hostile people on his way to Wales.

'Demobbed, Viney. It's short for demobilised. It means he won't have to be in the army any more. They call it returning to civvy street.

'Where's civvy street?' John asked, and Laura explained that it meant they could all go back to where they had been before the war started, although for many people that seemed unlikely.

For her it would mean having her husband back, and returning to St

Alban's, and meeting up with Dorothy again and taking up where they had left off. It also meant saying goodbye to Sybil, who had become very dear to her, and she knew that although the child was looking forward to being reunited with her parents, the wrench of parting from the Lucas family, and Viney in particular, would be hard to bear.

And then there was Sidney. Perhaps now it would be possible to trace his mother, although it would take some time. Britain was in a state of turmoil and it would take years to do all that needed to be done in straightening out the muddle of displaced families.

As for Laura, joyful though she was at the thought of having her husband back, she was also beset by anxiety. Having Neil home again would be like living with a stranger. It had been a long three years without him. Also, she wasn't sure she was ready to relinquish her place as head of the household. She had become used to being in charge and wouldn't relish being told what to do.

In the cities, in London in particular, people flocked into the streets, singing and dancing, servicemen and women still wearing the uniforms they had worn so proudly, while most civilians were dressed in shabby, well-worn garments dating from before the war.

On that day when victory was announced, there was a sense of pride and achievement which would help to see the country through as the daunting task of reconstruction began.

Things were quiet in Llanidris as Laura and her neighbours made rosettes to wear on their lapels, lovingly fashioned from red, white and blue ribbon. Flags were displayed in windows: the Union flag and the red dragon of Wales. Strings of bunting fluttered across the main street, in preparation for the celebratory party.

'Can we go to the party, Mum?' Young John wasn't sure what victory was, but he knew they'd be missing something if they couldn't go.

'Of course, love! We can't miss that!'

'What do people do at parties?'

'Well, we'll eat a lot of lovely food — and I've heard there might even be ice-cream. Won't that be wonderful?'

'I don't like ice-cream,' John told her, wrinkling his nose.

'You've never tasted it!' That was Mark, scornful as usual.

'Let's not squabble on such a happy day,' Laura chided. 'You don't remember ice-cream anyway, Mark; you were too young when they stopped making it. You'll love it, John, I promise you.'

'If he doesn't, can I have his share, Mum?' Mark, not at all chastened, was thinking of his stomach as usual.

The street party turned out to be a wonderful occasion, and even the occasional shower failed to dampen people's spirits. Trestle tables had been set up for the children, while their mothers bustled about serving blancmange and jelly and handing round cups of tea.

When everything had been cleared away, there were races, with prizes for the winners. The grown-ups had donated their precious sweet ration so that chocolate bars could be awarded to those who came first, second and third, with sherbet dabs for those who weren't placed. After years of privation it would have been too unkind for some children to have been turned away empty-handed.

That night an enormous bonfire was set alight in the park, with children and adults alike dancing round it as if they were taking part in some pagan ritual. It no longer mattered if the night sky was illuminated by the flames; no enemy bomber would be guided to Llanidris by the light.

Tired and dirty, the Lucas family finally made their way home to Lilac Lane, but they weren't a completely happy crew. Sidney was in tears because he was exhausted and it was long past his bedtime, and John was crying because Mark had relieved him of his last, jealously hoarded humbug, one of the sweets which had been given to the little ones in a small screw of paper after the party.

Surprisingly Sybil burst into tears as well. Usually Sybil was a stoic sort of child who buoyed everyone else up when things went wrong.

'What's the matter with the Lady Sybilla?' Laura teased, hoping to cheer her up.

'I don't want to go back to London,' she whispered.

'You don't mean that, love. I know you want to see Mummy again and I expect Daddy will be getting leave to come and see you both. It'll be lovely, being all together again.'

'I know, Auntie,' she sniffed, 'but I wish you were coming as well.'

'Oh, you won't get rid of us that easily, my girl,' Laura assured her brightly. 'One of these days we'll all be going back to St Alban's, and that isn't far from London, you know.'

'Or p'raps Sybil and me can go to

boarding-school together,' announced Viney, who had been reading some of Angela Brazil's school stories.

And pigs might fly, Laura thought, remembering the size of a policeman's wage packet. But she simply smiled down at her two girls and said, 'Come on, let's get you lot in. Don't worry about having a proper wash, just a lick and a promise will do. Then it's off to bed with you.'

The crisis was over momentarily, but the moment of parting couldn't be put off for ever, and the day came when the family accompanied Sybil to the station to see her off.

Sybil boarded the train with an expression on her face suggestive of one climbing into a tumbril on her way to the guillotine. Laura found herself holding on to John and Sidney, who were attempting to follow the older boys, who had wandered off to inspect the engine.

'You've got your sandwiches, haven't you?' Laura asked again in an attempt

101

to fill the silence.

'Yes, Auntie, and thank you very much for my comic.'

'That's all right, dear. Mummy will be at the other end to meet you; be sure to give her my love, won't you?'

'Don't forget to write to me, Viney.'

'I'll write every day,' Viney promised.

'Perhaps not every day,' Laura cautioned. 'Stamps cost money.'

The engine began to get up steam and she delivered some last-minute admonitions. 'Remember what I've told you, Sybil — don't talk to any strange men, and don't stick your head out of the window when the train's going through a tunnel, or you may get it cut off!'

'I promise, Auntie. Goodbye!'

'Goodbye! Goodbye!'

So Sybil disappeared out of their lives, leaving them all feeling bereft.

'Do you know what?' Viney whispered to her mother as they made their way home, with the boys running in front of them, noisily imitating aeroplanes.

'Matthew kissed Sybil before we left the house.' Viney giggled from behind her hand. 'I think he's in love with her, Mum.'

'Don't be silly. He's only twelve years old,' Laura replied, but even at that age, she knew, hearts can break, and her own heart went out to her kindly, sensitive son.

★  ★  ★

Neil Lucas came home, thinner than Laura remembered him, with a great deal of grey in his dark hair and wearing a ghastly 'demob' suit that hung loosely on his tall frame.

They embraced awkwardly and then he released her to look at his children, standing all in a row beneath a clumsy home-made banner which read **Welcome Home Dad**.

'You've all grown so much,' he marvelled. 'Shot up like trees, you have. I wouldn't have recognised any of you if I'd met you in the street.'

'It has been three years,' Laura murmured, wishing there was something she could do or say to break the ice. They had all looked forward so much to this day and now they were standing about like strangers, fumbling for words.

'What have you all been doing?' Neil asked at last, and that opened the floodgates. He sank down into his mother's old wing chair and let the chatter flow over him while Laura went to make him a cup of tea.

Before his arrival, Laura had given the children strict warnings about what to do and say — or rather, what *not* to do.

'Don't ask him about the prison camp,' she stressed. 'He may not want to talk about it. And don't expect him to do things with you just at first. Coming home is bound to feel strange when he's been away for so long. Just give him time to make the adjustment, all right?'

Unfortunately she hadn't been able

to cover every eventuality. Neil had been back for less than two hours when a rift opened between them, a gulf so wide that she doubted if it could ever be mended.

It began when Viney was just showing her father the new jumper Laura had knitted after pulling down an old one of her own. A loud wail from overhead signalled that Sidney was awake.

Neil's head swivelled to the ceiling. 'What's that?'

'Oh, that's our Sid,' Viney told him. 'Shall I fetch him, Mum?'

'Yes, all right, love, but be careful lifting him out of his cot. Don't drop him, will you?'

Neil took a long look at the laughing baby who Viney proudly presented to him, and his face took on a shuttered look. He lit another cigarette and got to his feet.

'I'm off out for a walk.'

'Can I come, Dad?' Mark asked eagerly, but Neil ignored him and strode out, letting the door bang shut behind him.

'He's mean! I only wanted to go for a walk, and he didn't even answer,' the boy complained to his mother.

'He's not used to having children around. You must give him time to settle in.'

Mark wasn't to be mollified. 'It was all right till that baby came down. He wasn't expecting to have a smelly baby here when he came home.'

'Sidney doesn't smell!' Viney retorted, but Mark only slammed out of the room, his face set in mutinous lines.

Laura sank down on the sofa, her thoughts in a whirl. Had Mark hit the nail on the head? Surely she must have told Neil about Sidney?

It was with a sinking feeling that she realised that she might not have said enough.

In the beginning she hadn't expected the baby to become a permanent fixture in the home. Reubena might have turned up again at any moment to claim her infant, full of excuses about where she'd been, and why.

When writing to her husband, Laura had tried to avoid mentioning things which might worry or upset him. He had to know that things were difficult on the home front, yet she had thought it would comfort him to know they were coping well. Her letters had been full of what the children were up to; she had mentioned their little successes, but had carefully glossed over Mark's problems. All that could wait until Neil was restored to them, she had decided.

Now he was back, seemingly upset at the sight of Sidney, and she didn't know how to handle it. Was he afraid that having a baby to see to would keep her too busy to pay attention to him?

She would have to tackle the subject as soon as possible, and tell him that the authorities would have to try to trace some relative who could take the child; a grandmother, perhaps, or an aunt. The war was over now and her responsibility was at an end.

The hours passed, with no sign of Neil. The welcome home supper she'd so lovingly planned was drying up in the oven, and the children had been sent to bed, disappointed.

Laura had an idea that he would be in the Red Dragon, being plied with drinks by the locals. Well, there was nothing wrong with that, as long as he didn't mean to make a habit of it. She only hoped he wouldn't come rolling home like a drunken sailor.

However, her fears were realised when, shortly after closing time, the door flew open and there stood Neil swaying on the threshold. Biting her lip, she went forward to guide him in.

'Good little wifie, waiting to welcome hubby home,' he sneered.

'Come and sit down now, dear . . . '

'Don't you 'dear' me! I know what you've been up to while I've been gone!'

She stared at him. 'I don't know what you mean.'

'Is that so? Then what do you call that kid upstairs? Stanley, or whatever his name is? While the cat's away, the mice will play, eh?'

Laura's heart sank.

'Neil Lucas! You can't be suggesting that Sidney . . . oh, I can't believe this! You think that I'd actually stoop so low as to have an affair while you were a prisoner of war for all those years?'

'Wouldn't be the first time a woman went astray with her husband behind the wire,' he mumbled.

'Well, that's not what happened here!' Laura snapped.

'Then what's he doing here, large as life? Tell me that, eh?' He lumbered to his feet and began roaming round the room, sweeping books off the table in a fit of anger as he went.

Alerted by the commotion, the children had got up and were huddled together at the top of the stairs, looking worried.

'Go back to bed, everything's all right,' Laura cried when she saw them.

'Take the others into your room, Mark, and make sure they stay there. Matthew, I want you to run up to the vicarage and fetch Mr Smart here. Tell him it's urgent.'

'But, Mum, look at the time!'

'Never mind that! Just do as you're told.'

Scared, Matthew ran off into the darkness.

It seemed like an eternity before she heard a car stop at the gate; Matthew must have convinced the vicar that there was indeed an emergency in Lilac Lane for him to have used still-precious petrol on the journey.

Mr Smart took in the situation at a glance. The condition of the room, the look on Laura's white face, the man sprawled in a chair, uttering foul language.

'It's Sidney,' Laura explained. 'My husband thinks I . . . ' Sobs choked her and she was unable to continue.

'Oh, well, that's easily put right,' Mr Smart soothed her, understanding the situation at once, 'but it's useless trying to do anything while he's in this state. One too many in the Red Dragon, I suppose. Only to be expected after all he's been through. I'll explain things to him in the morning, and if he won't believe me, there's plenty of folk in Llanidris who can tell him all about young Reubena, if only he's prepared to listen.'

'That's what I thought, Vicar, but I don't know what to do about him tonight. I'm afraid he'll frighten the children, if nothing worse,' she sighed.

'Then I'll take him back with me for the night, and if he gives me any trouble I'll call out Dr Foy to give him a sedative. In fact, I believe I'll do that in any case. Let's get him out to the car now. Can you take his other arm, Matthew? That's right . . . '

\* \* \*

It was a contrite Neil who arrived home at eleven o'clock the next morning, desperate to make amends.

'I'm so sorry,' he mumbled into Laura's hair. 'Can you ever forgive me, love?'

'There's nothing to forgive,' she murmured, thinking it best not to dwell on her hurt and outrage. 'Surely I told you about Reubena and her baby in one of my letters?'

'I seem to remember something, ages ago,' he conceded, 'but I assumed he'd been taken away by his mother, like the little girl you fostered. Hearing about evacuees in a letter when you're far away isn't the same as coming face to face with a flesh and blood child in your own home.'

There was a lot more that Laura might have said, particularly about not jumping to conclusions, but she bit back the words, knowing that if she wanted her marriage to succeed she would have to be patient. Unfortunately, patience wasn't her strong suit!

She reminded herself of that a week later when she learned that Neil had made certain decisions without consulting her.

'I suppose we should be thinking about getting back to St Alban's,' she remarked, when they were strolling together through the woods, enjoying the evening air. Sidney and John had been left with Mrs Jenkins, who was 'happy to oblige' as she put it when Laura asked as if she'd mind keeping an eye on them for an hour.

'I've decided we'll stay here, Laura. I did a lot of thinking when I was in the camp, and I know I don't want to go back to police work. I'm not even sure I'm fit for it now.'

'Then what will you do?'

'I'm going to be a gamekeeper, like my father before me. I spent hours helping him as a boy, so I know what's involved. That hush-hush government department has been moved back to London and the Hall is being handed back to the Morgans. I called to see old Morgan when I was passing through London and he's agreed to take me on.

Getting the place back in shape won't be easy, but he's determined to try.'

'But I was looking forward to going back to England, Neil — seeing Dorothy and all the familiar places. And Viney's expecting to see Sybil again as well.'

He was shaking his head. 'You haven't seen the devastation caused by the bombing there, Laura. Housing is almost impossible to find, and priority will be given to homeless families. As people with a house of our own here, we'll be at the bottom of the list — if we even get on it at all. No, it's best we stay here. In any case, I've already accepted this job, so that's all there is to it.'

Laura had no choice but to accept his decision. Neil was home, and she had to relinquish her position as head of the family.

So they all settled down to what they hoped would be a happy future in Lilac Lane. The war was over and they were together again. So many people had lost everything, but they were among the lucky ones, safe and well and living in pleasant surroundings. Who could wish for anything more?

# 1953

In a house filled mainly with men and boys, the teenaged Viney Lucas often wished she had a sister to confide in. As that wasn't possible, her thoughts often went to her wartime companion, Sybil Waite. Although the girls had sworn to write to each other, their good intentions hadn't lasted. A few stilted letters, consisting mainly of such lifeless prose as 'How are you? I am fine,' had been sent off, with the gaps between writing getting longer and longer, and then the correspondence had faded away.

However, their mothers had continued to exchange Christmas cards and when Viney decided she wanted to get in touch again, Sybil's address was easy to find.

An answer came by return of post, scattered with exclamation marks.

'So lovely to hear from you! What

have you been up to? Write at once and tell me everything!'

By 'everything' Viney supposed Sybil meant boys, but there was nothing to tell. That was the disadvantage of attending an all-girls school, especially one where the headmistress had announced that on pain of death no girl was to be seen walking home with a pupil from the nearby boys' grammar school.

'Well, not death, exactly,' Viney wrote, 'but detention anyway, and a letter sent home.'

'Isn't it stupid?' Sybil wrote back. 'In some countries girls our age are married with a few kids. And look at Juliet!! At least you've got brothers, Viney. Can't they introduce you to their mates?'

But Viney didn't want to suffer Mark's remorseless teasing, so she left well alone and decided to concentrate on swotting for her O-levels instead

Lilac Lane was bulging at the seams. Four years previously, to her father's delight and her mother's amazement, a new baby had arrived. Aidan was a handsome child and both parents doted on him. By the time he was old enough to move out of his parents' bedroom his brothers insisted that they would leave home if they had to share a room with the little devil, so Neil was forced to convert the attic into a room for his grown-up sons.

'You can have it for a sewing-room or something when they leave home,' he told Laura, who smiled vaguely and said nothing. If there was anything she hated it was sewing. She used her Singer treadle machine to do the mending and that was quite enough for her.

'So Aidan's sharing with John,' Viney wrote, 'and you should hear John grumble! It's Sidney Porter all over again. Do you remember him? Poor John used to get his toys broken by that baby, and now he's going through it again with Aidan and his precious records.

'Sidney stayed with us for quite a while, until some old aunt came out of the woodwork and gave him a home. I never did hear what happened to Reubena, although rumour has it that she eloped with an American soldier and went off to Toledo, Ohio.'

'Tell me about the other boys,' Sybil ordered. 'I bet Mark's quite good looking, isn't he?'

'Good looking? Are you out of your mind? He's covered in grease half the time now he's training to be a mechanic. He's even got an old wreck of a car which he's trying to restore. It's an Austin Seven. Dad calls it the flying biscuit box.

'If anybody in our family is good looking, it's Matt. Did I mention that he's working with Dad, up at the Hall? He likes the open air and he keeps rabbiting on about emigrating to Australia and working in everlasting sunshine.

'It's too early to tell what John will turn out like. At the moment he's spotty and speccy, but Mum says that doesn't matter. He's going to be somebody, is our John, she says. She says he's got more brains than the rest of us put together.'

Sybil had now abandoned her childish dream of marrying into the nobility and had set her sights on a doctor instead. 'Not that I've found one yet,' she wrote, 'but if I get into nursing school I'll meet plenty of them, and then we'll see.'

'You'll have to wait a while, then,' Viney cautioned. 'One of my schoolfriends has a sister who's a nurse. She says that probationers aren't even allowed to speak to doctors. One of the consultants was on the ward when she took a phone call for him and she had to tell Sister so that she could tell him, even though the man was standing right beside her.'

Viney had eagerly soaked up all this information because she hoped to become a nurse herself. If she did well in her O-levels she meant to apply to several different hospitals so she had a choice of where to go when she was old enough.

'We MUST sign on at the same place,' Sybil insisted. 'Tell me where you want to go and I'll write to the hospitals for information.'

'You could do children's nursing after you qualify,' Laura suggested when informed of these plans. 'I've watched you with Aidan and you're good with babies. Or you could do midwifery. The sky's the limit if you decide to go on with more training.'

* * *

Laura was happier than she'd ever been in her life before. On one hand she had seen her older boys grow into fine young men, launched on satisfying careers, and now her daughter was well on her way to making a worthwhile contribution to the world. On the other hand she still had John and Aidan to enjoy for some years yet. John was a gangly teenager who was already showing signs of achieving great things, and Aidan — well, he was just Aidan. She wondered sometimes if she was too lenient with him, because he was a naughty young rascal, but perhaps that was the result of being a later baby.

Neil, too, seemed happy. 'I'm glad now that I didn't insist on us going back to St Alban's,' she wrote to Dorothy. 'After all that time shut up in the prison camp he can't stand to be confined. He still needs to get out and walk for miles, so being a gamekeeper is just what he needs.'

Laura was proud of the way her husband looked in his working clothes. He wore a brown coat of rough tweed, a relic from before the war which was so well made that it would probably last forever. With his corduroy trousers tucked into stout wellies, and a tweed hat on his head, he looked every inch the country gentleman.

Young Matt enjoyed the work, too, although he annoyed his father by saying that gamekeepers were going out of fashion, which was why he was thinking about emigrating.

'It's not like it was in Grandpa's day,' he explained, as if they didn't know. 'Hordes of titled people having shooting parties and slaughtering birds by the hundreds.'

'Mr Morgan has been forced to diversify,' Neil muttered.

Hit hard by post-war taxation, the owner of the estate now raised game for market. The only thing that hadn't changed was that his employees spent much of their time getting rid of vermin. This distressed Viney who kept saying that wild animals deserved to live too, but her mother told her to keep her opinions to herself and not make critical remarks about their livelihood.

'There's more than one kind of vermin,' Matthew muttered, when he came home one evening after a particularly trying day. 'Can you put tea back a bit, Mum? Dad's going to be late. He's gone up to the Hall to speak to Mr Morgan.'

'Something wrong, then?'

'You could say that. We've got poachers.'

'Is that all? That's nothing new. I don't think the Morgans have ever worried too much about one of the locals snaring a rabbit for the pot. It's not like the old days, when land-owners set mantraps and then shipped off the offenders to Botany Bay.'

'This is worse, Mum. Gangs of men robbing us blind, taking game to sell in the cities. And the worst of it is, we can't do a thing unless we catch them in the act. Dad says he'd like to pepper them all with buckshot, but then he'd be up before the magistrates himself and probably sent down for a stretch!'

Laura laughed, knowing it was all talk. Neil would no more shoot a poacher than fly in the air.

'I expect it'll all come out in the wash,' she said. Neil would do his job to the best of his ability, and for her part she would maintain a comfortable home for him to return to when his day's work was done.

So in the spring of 1953 life went on as usual for the Lucas family, and it seemed to Viney that nothing would ever change. Oh, she would go off to train as a nurse eventually, but the rest of the family would still be here, waiting for her to come back to them.

She had no way of knowing that disaster was waiting to strike, something which would affect her more deeply than the war had done. Her whole life was about to be thrown into disarray.

⋆　⋆　⋆

Having come safely through the war it was ironic and extremely sad that Laura Lucas should develop serious health problems as the new decade progressed. Occupied with their own concerns, the family failed to notice how breathless she was when walking uphill or going upstairs, and she herself attributed her occasional sharp chest pains to indigestion.

'Are you all right, *bach*?' Mrs Jenkins next door had come out to peg her washing on the line and had seen Laura doing the same thing. At least, the basket of wet sheets was there on the grass, and some pillow-cases were already fluttering on the line, but Laura was standing with her hands clasped under her chin, looking white and strained.

When she didn't answer the older woman squeezed through the gap in the boundary fence, repeating her question as she came.

'I came over a bit faint,' Laura muttered. 'I'll be all right in a minute.'

'You don't look all right to me,' Mrs Jenkins protested. 'I'll help you into the house and then we'll send for the doctor. And never mind them sheets,' she went on. 'I'll see to them in a minute.'

With Laura stretched out on the sofa Mrs Jenkins ran out to the lane and flagged down a passing cyclist, who was dispatched to the doctor's house.

By the time Neil Lucas came home, tramping his muddy boots all over the clean kitchen floor, the doctor had been and gone.

Neil frowned when he saw their neighbour at the sink, filling a basin with hot water. 'Where's Laura? I was expecting to find my dinner waiting. I haven't got long.'

'You'll have to make do with bread and cheese then, because Laura's not well. I expect you can find your way to the larder, can't you?'

There was no love lost between Mrs Jenkins and Neil Lucas, whom she regarded as a demanding brute of a man. His wife made excuses for him, of course, saying that he'd been a lovely man before the war and it was his life in the prison camp that had changed him, but Mrs Jenkins didn't believe a word of it. He wasn't the only one who had suffered in those years, not by a long chalk, and now it was time to move on.

'Bread and cheese! What kind of dinner is that for a working man?' Neil exploded. 'I'll give her not well! She has nothing to do all day while I'm out working to support us all! It's the least she can do to provide my meals on time.'

Mrs Jenkins controlled her temper with difficulty.

'The doctor has been, Mr Lucas. Apparently your wife has to go to Morriston for tests of some sort, but there, she'll tell you all about it, I'm sure. And please take your boots off before you go marching in. You're spreading mud everywhere. Have you no consideration?'

'If looks could kill I'd have been ready for the undertaker right there and then, our Glad,' she explained to her daughter later, 'but he did what he was told, for a wonder.'

'What is it then, Mam?'

'It's her heart, I think. The plain fact is, the poor soul is worn out, looking after all that lot, washing and ironing and cooking and cleaning, and he doesn't make it easy on her, the way he orders her about.'

'What's wrong with Viney, then? Don't she give her mam a hand?'

'I daresay she would, given the chance, but she's got that Aidan hanging round her neck all the time, see? Into mischief every minute of the day, that child is, and not a word spoken by him, for all he's almost four. It'll come as a relief to the pair of them when he's old enough to go to school.' She sighed. 'That's if they'll have him there.'

'A bit simple, isn't he?' Gladys commented. 'What's to become of him if his mother goes? I can't see Neil Lucas having the patience to put up with his tantrums for long.'

Lying down next door, Laura was thinking much the same thing. The doctor had been very kind, calmly brushing off her frantic questions as to whether it was her heart and if she was going to die.

'Let's just wait and see, shall we? You'll be having some tests which should tell us more, and meanwhile I'll prescribe something to help you along. You're to stay lying down for the rest of the day, and I'll call again tomorrow.'

So kind Mrs Jenkins had seen to the washing, even going so far as to mop up in the wash-house and, best of all, had taken young Aidan round to her house for the afternoon.

'I'll give him his tea and bring him back at bedtime,' she'd said. 'Viney can get tea for the rest of them, I expect.'

Now the house was silent, but for the sound of the clock ticking.

'Aidan,' Laura thought as she drifted off to sleep. 'Where did I go wrong?'

Aidan was one of the thousands of babies who had come into being after their fathers returned from the war. He was a lovely child with the face of an angel — when he wasn't crying, that is. He suffered from colic which even frequent doses of gripe water failed to cure, and there were times when sleep-deprived Laura felt like leaving him on the church steps for some other person to care for. Then she was consumed with guilt, for what proper mother could feel like that about her own baby?

Luckily Viney delighted in walking through the village pushing Aidan in his pram, when, miraculously, the movement seemed to soothe him. This gave Laura some much-needed time to get on with other things.

'What if I die?' Laura asked herself now. 'What's to become of them all? What will happen to Aidan?'

When he had reached the age of three without ever uttering a word, although there was certainly nothing wrong with his lungs, she had taken him to the doctor to find out what was wrong.

'I wondered if he's deaf,' she'd ventured, 'or . . . ' She'd left the words unsaid, somehow believing that if she put her fears into words they might come true.

'He's certainly not deaf,' the doctor had told her. 'A bit lazy, perhaps. Let's put it this way; he's a late arrival in a household of other children, who probably wait on him hand and foot. Isn't that the case?'

'Well, my daughter . . . '

'I expect she dotes on the little fellow and he's only to put out a hand to have her put something in it at once. He never has to ask, and therefore doesn't need to speak.'

'But he's always into mischief, Doctor. Every time I turn around he's doing something he shouldn't.'

The doctor had glanced at Aidan, sitting on his mother's lap looking as if butter wouldn't melt in his mouth.

'Boys will be boys, Mrs Lucas. Rest assured, there's nothing wrong with your son that time won't cure. Once he goes to school he'll find other avenues for his energy, and he'll soon start chattering away when he mixes with others his own age.'

He wasn't an unkind man, but he

saw too many children who were far less healthy than Aidan Lucas. Children with rickets or tuberculosis or deformities. He had no time to waste on one who was simply a little slow.

Laura had tramped home, feeling let down. Was she being silly? She must tell Viney not to dance attendance on him so much, although to be truthful she was glad of the peace and quiet which resulted, and the girl seemed happy enough to look after him. A real little mother, she was.

'Mum? Are you all right?'

Laura opened her eyes to find Viney looking anxiously down at her.

'Course I am, love. Just having forty winks, that's all. Where is everybody?'

'John's playing football with his mates, and the others aren't in from work yet. Aidan's still round at Mrs Jenkins' house. Shall I go and fetch him?'

Laura sighed. 'I suppose you'd better. She's had him most of the day. Heaven knows what he's been up to.'

However, at that moment Mrs Jenkins walked into the house, leading Aidan by the hand.

'Here we are, then! I saw Viney come in, so I thought I'd bring him home. He's had his tea. Ate everything on his plate, he did.'

'I hope you've been a good boy,' Laura murmured, seeing that her son was wearing his most angelic smile.

'Good as gold!' Mrs Jenkins nodded. 'Not a bit of trouble, he wasn't. He played with my button box, lining them up like little soldiers. All the red ones together in one place and the blue ones in another.'

Laura shuddered. Given Aidan's habit of putting everything in his mouth it was a wonder he hadn't swallowed a button and choked on it, but he was obviously all right so she said nothing.

'And what about you, Mrs Lucas? Had a nice rest, have you? Pain all gone now?'

'Yes, thank you.'

'I'll be off home, then. Send one of

the children round if there's anything you need.' She bustled off, looking virtuous.

Aidan immediately went to the shelf where the biscuit barrel was kept and pointed, grunting.

'Say biscuit,' Viney prompted. He merely grunted louder.

'Bis-kit,' she repeated, and he let out a roar of indignation.

'Better give him one,' Laura said. She knew she shouldn't give in to the little devil but the last thing she wanted now was a confrontation.

\* \* \*

Neil Lucas leaned back in the leather chair, looking as though he'd been clubbed. His wife sat beside him, head down, hands folded in her lap.

'But she can be cured, Doctor, can't she? You can give her pills or something, surely?'

'Yes, Mr Lucas, we can certainly give her medication to deal with various aspects of her condition, but you have to understand that heart disease is a serious business. Given proper care and treatment your wife may be able to jog along for quite some time. I'll provide the latter, but the former is up to you.'

They're talking over my head as if I wasn't here, Laura thought dully.

They had come to learn the results of the tests they had run on her at the big hospital, Neil grumbling about the time lost from his work, and the news hadn't been good. She was suffering from some alarming form of heart ailment which she barely understood because of the medical jargon the doctor used. Perhaps she hadn't listened properly because she was so worried; Neil might be able to fill in the gaps when they got home.

She wished her mother was still alive. There were feelings she wanted to share which could not be voiced to Neil or the children.

She felt so tired these days that the thought of slipping away into nothingness was inviting, yet on the other hand she didn't want to die. What would Neil do without her? And the children! The older boys would be all right, but she needed to be there for Aidan. With his problems he'd have a hard enough row to hoe when he was grown but it was now that he needed a mother to guide him.

'Please, God,' she whispered, 'let me be able to carry on.'

She came to with a start, realising that Neil was frowning at her, and she reached out to accept the paper the doctor had torn off his prescription pad.

'One of those, night and morning, Mrs Lucas, and you must try to get more rest. I want you to spend the afternoons lying down. Is that clear?'

'Yes, Doctor, I'll try.'

⋆ ⋆ ⋆

Viney stared at her father in disbelief. 'I'll do what I can to help Mum, you know I will, but the boys will have to help. I've got important exams coming up, and you want me to do all the washing and cooking. There aren't enough hours in a day.'

'You can get up earlier and make breakfast for us all, and put together packed lunches. Do what your mother does and put the wash in to soak overnight, then you can get it done first thing. All it takes is a bit of organisation.'

Viney bit her lip, saying nothing, but as soon as she had the chance she went next door to ask Mrs Jenkins what she thought about it all.

'Dad just has no idea!' she burst out.

'Men never do, *bach*,' the neighbour sniffed. 'What is it this time, then?'

'He thinks I can do the wash before I go to school. I'd have to get up at four o'clock if I did that!'

She thought of the hours her mother spent rocking the lever back and forth on the Acme washer, then rinsing the garments in the galvanised tub and running them through the mangle before staggering out to the line to peg them out. All that was almost a full day's occupation when you were looking after seven people, especially when three of them were men who had dirty jobs.

'Perhaps your mam could send the wash out,' Mrs Jenkins said helpfully. 'The Daffodil Laundry picks up and delivers every week. Let them take the bigger items and you just do the smalls at home.'

'It's a lovely idea, Mrs Jenkins, but I don't see Dad agreeing to it. I might be able to do it after school, but I'm afraid that Mum would get on with it herself while I was away. You know what the women are like hereabouts; if the sheets aren't on the line by ten o'clock you're branded a lazy good-for-nothing.'

'If that's how they feel, let them come and give a hand! But there, your mam is a proud woman. I suppose she wouldn't want to accept charity. As I see it, your only alternative is to stay home from school on Monday mornings and just get on with it.'

Viney did this two weeks running, earning stern reproofs from her form mistress. 'This is an important year for you, Viney, don't you realise that?'

'Yes, Miss Rhys-Jones.'

'You say you want become a nurse and we have high hopes for you, but it will all come to nothing if you fail your state exams. You can't afford to miss school now that all the classes are doing revision. It's all very well to swot at home, but the staff are attempting to fill the gaps in your knowledge and to answer questions. All this is vital to your future, child.'

Viney knew that what the teacher said was true, and she also knew that it was useless to argue. Answering back was likely to earn her an hour's detention, which she could ill afford. If Dad's tea wasn't on the table when he came home from work she would be in trouble!

As things turned out, getting the tea

was the least of her worries when she arrived home. Aidan was bawling and she found him lying on the kitchen floor, drumming his heels in a full-scale tantrum.

'Thanks goodness you've come!' Thirteen-year-old John gazed up at her, looking pale and anxious. 'He's been like this for ages and I can't make him stop!'

Viney looked around. 'What's going on? Where's Mum?'

'She's sick again. I had to go and call the ambulance. They've taken her to the cottage hospital.'

Viney's stomach churned. 'Where's Dad? Does he know about this?'

John studied his boots. 'He's not home from work yet.'

'I can see that, but surely you went to find him?'

'There's no point in going. He could be anywhere on the estate, Viney, you know that.'

There was some truth in that, but even so, it wasn't good enough. What if it was serious this time? Neil Lucas would want to be at his wife's side.

'I'll go and look for Dad,' she decided. 'He might be in the office at this time of day. I'll go there first.'

'Who's going to look after Aidan?' John bleated.

'It's either you or me, John, and since you've not seen fit to get Dad, I'll go and you'll have to babysit. Give him a biscuit or something to shut him up.'

She rushed out of the door, followed by their cries of indignation. Couldn't they understand that Mum came first in all this?

Luckily Neil was in the ivy-covered shed that was known as the game-keeper's office. He looked up from his ledger when she approached, giving her a vague smile.

'Hello, love! What brings you here? On your way home from school, are you?'

She hated to put a damper on this rare good mood, but there was no help for it.

'They've taken Mum to the cottage hospital, Dad. John said she had a bad turn and he had to get the ambulance.'

Neil closed the leather-bound book with a bang.

'You get back home and see to the lads. I'll be right behind you.'

Viney looked at him fearfully. 'What are you going to do, Dad?'

'I'm going up to the Hall to see Mr Morgan. First off, I want to ring the hospital and see what the story is. After that, I want to borrow the brake in case I need to get over there in a hurry. Don't worry, I'll be home to have a wash before I go anywhere; that's if I do have to set off right away. If things aren't that serious, they'll probably say I have to wait until visiting hours.'

'But John said . . . '

'Never mind what John said. He's just a boy, worried about his mother. Now just do as I say, there's a good girl.'

Reluctantly Viney sped home. She looked back over her shoulder at one point and was reassured to see her father hurrying up the road towards the Hall. He was in charge now, which made her feel much better.

By the time their father came home the older boys were also there, grumbling because there hadn't been a cooked meal waiting for them. Viney had handed out bread and cheese and when Aidan threw his share on the floor and began to whine, she rounded on him so fiercely that for once he stopped fussing and stared at her crossly.

'Is Mum all right?' Matt asked when Neil came in, and they were all taken back when he shook his head grimly.

'The doctors say we should come at once. Your mother's asking to see us. Get tidied up and out to the brake, will you?'

'I'll go and see if Mrs Jenkins can take Aidan,' Viney began, but he shook his head.

'No, love. Your Mum particularly wants to see Aidan.'

And that was when Viney knew that something was very wrong indeed, and that after today, nothing was ever going to be the same again.

# Sad Days . . .

'Come here, all of you. Let me give you a kiss.' Laura's voice was weak as she stared at the anxious little group ranged around the foot of her bed. Aidan was squirming in his father's arms, not understanding what was happening, but the rest of them were white-faced and shocked.

When each of them had given and received a hug and a kiss, she asked the boys to wait outside while she had a word with Viney. That done, she turned to her husband as Viney stumbled out of the ward, her eyes blinded by tears.

'What did she say to you?' Matt demanded. 'What's going on in there?'

Viney could only shake her head wordlessly.

'Promise me you'll look after Aidan,' her mother had whispered.

'I will, Mum.'

'I don't just mean while I'm in here, love. I mean always. You'll never leave him, will you?' and once again Viney had given her word.

Later, when she was lying in bed at home, that scene went round and round in her head. The boys were all in bed, but she was too upset to settle. Matt had driven them all home but Neil had remained with his wife, which seemed ominous. They didn't let people stay after visiting hours unless something was terribly wrong.

It was almost breakfast-time before their father returned, having caught an early workmen's bus which had dropped him at the crossroads. He came into the kitchen without speaking and sank down at the table with his head in his hands.

'She's gone,' he said at last. 'I was with her at the end. It was very peaceful.'

Viney put an arm round his shaking shoulders, not knowing what else to do. John began to cry, his harsh sobs filling the room. The older boys said nothing, for what good were words at a time like this? Talking could come later.

Suddenly a burst of loud laughter erupted as Aidan skipped into the room. His eyes gleaming, he reached up for the milk jug, fumbled, and sent the contents flying all over the table. He tugged at his father's sleeve, pointing gleefully.

'Get that brat out of here!' Neil roared, getting up so quickly that Viney stepped back hurriedly to avoid being knocked over. 'You heard what I said, girl! Take him out of my sight before I give him the walloping he deserves!'

'He didn't mean any harm, Dad. It was an accident.'

'Is that so? Then let me tell you this: if it wasn't for that little devil your mother would still be alive today. She wore herself out looking after him and his antics, and I for one will never forgive him!'

He stormed out of the house, slamming the door behind him. His family exchanged uneasy glances.

'He's upset. He didn't mean it,' Viney said, seeing John's white face.

'I expect he did,' Mark put in. 'I heard her telling Aidan the other day that he'd be the death of her, and that's the honest truth.'

'She told *you* that often enough,' Matt scoffed. 'It's the sort of thing mothers say when their kids drive them wild.'

'I know that, I'm not stupid. But let's face it, none of us was a patch on Aidan.'

Sadly Viney fetched the cloth and began to mop up the milk, which by now was staining the red tiles under the table. She wished she could ask the doctors why her mother had died. She'd had heart trouble, of course, but why did people get that? Stress was supposed to be bad for you, but if that was the only reason, the whole population of Britain should be in a bad way after their experiences in the war!

Aidan *was* a difficult child, but there

were far worse cases than her little brother, such as the two evacuees from London who'd managed to burn down Mrs Roberts' chicken house when they'd hidden in there to smoke stolen cigarettes.

Viney was shocked by what her father had come out with, and even more upset by the fact that he'd raised his hand to Aidan, even though he'd let it fall to his side before he'd actually delivered the blow.

As younger children all of them had been smacked after doing wrong, as their parents believed that it was a question of spare the rod and spoil the child. However, Neil had left that to his wife, preferring to rule by word of mouth instead. When he spoke, his children listened.

\* \* \*

The next few days passed in a blur for Viney. The funeral had been held, and her mother had been laid to rest in the churchyard close to Neil's parents.

Laura was English; did she mind being buried here among all these Welsh folk, far away from the place where she had been born and raised? Wanting to believe that her mother was even now looking down on them from Heaven, Viney decided that she would be glad to be close to the family she had been forced to leave behind. They could all go to visit the grave and when Aidan was a little older Viney would talk to him about his mother and help him pick flowers to place there.

It was on Sunday that the blow fell. She was ironing a blouse for school and suddenly became aware that her father was looming over her, frowning.

'What's all this, then? Ironing on a Sunday?'

'Just my school blouse for tomorrow, Dad. I didn't have time before.'

'You won't be needing that any more, Viney, not for school, at any rate. I suppose it'll do for around the house.'

'What do you mean, Dad?'

'Isn't it obvious? You're the woman of the house now. You'll be staying home to look after things. Your book-learning days are over, and not before time, a girl of sixteen.'

Viney was horrified. 'But I want to be a nurse, Dad! I've wanted that for ever so long. That's why I've been swotting so hard for my exams. The head says I'm sure to be accepted if I get good results.'

'No chance of that now. You're needed here, my girl.'

The tears coursed down Viney's cheeks as she tried to find words to convince him.

'I'll do everything I can before and after school, Dad, if you'll only let me sit the exams and finish out my year. Please, Dad.'

'And what good will that do? You wouldn't be able to go into training even if you did pass, so what's the use? You're needed to run the house now your poor mother's gone.'

Resentment boiled up in Viney. 'We'd

be able to manage if the boys would pull their weight, Dad! They could learn to clean their rooms and help with the washing-up, even take their turn with the cooking if I showed them what to do.'

'Now you're being silly. All that's woman's work. Men go out into the world and provide for the family; women provide a comfortable home for them to come back to at night. Besides, I don't hold with so much education for girls. If I let you go to this hospital of yours you'd only throw it all up some day to get married and it would all be wasted. No man worth his salt would let his wife go out to work, let me tell you.'

Viney wanted to scream that she, too, wanted to go out into the world and see what life was all about. And what if she never did get married, what was she supposed to do then with no qualifications? She could just see herself, twenty years from now, looking after an ageing father, or acting as an unpaid drudge in the home of a married brother.

Her thoughts turned to her youngest brother. She had promised Mum she'd look after Aidan, but she hadn't realised that it would come down to this.

The next morning she marched up to the school anyway, taking Aidan with her in his pushchair because there was nobody to leave him with. Her headmistress greeted her with surprise.

'Why aren't you in class, Viney? Weren't you listening when I stressed how important these next few weeks are to your future career?'

'*This* is my future career, Miss Thomas,' Viney said bitterly, indicating Aidan. 'Dad says I have to leave school to take Mum's place in the house.'

She poured out her misery while the headmistress listened sympathetically. How many times had she heard similar stories of promising girls being made to give up their education because parents had a different vision for their future? 'Mair is needed at home,' a father would say, or, 'We're taking Marged into the shop. No point paying an assistant when there's one of our own to do the job.'

'Perhaps I might suggest a compromise,' she ventured now. 'We'll ask your father to let you sit your exams as planned. Oh, I realise that you can't attend school, but I could ask your teachers to set you some revision so you could work at home. It won't be easy, I know, but it's better than nothing.'

'But Dad says that nursing is out,' Viney argued.

'And we must accept his decision, I'm afraid. But at least if you pass you'll have some qualifications behind you that will stand you in good stead if you ever do become an old maid, as you fear!'

The woman smiled ruefully. Her fiancé had been killed in the war and she had no thoughts of finding a new love, but she was aware of society's view of single women.

Hope dawned on Viney's face. With

the headmistress on her side, Dad might listen.

Miss Gwyneth Thomas took a long look at the man seated across from her desk and liked what she saw. He had the bronzed complexion of a man who worked outdoors, and had his eyes not been filled with the pain of bereavement, he would be handsome.

She understood that he had spent some years in a German prisoner of war camp but if this were the case then he had come through it remarkably well. It was a tragedy that he had lost his wife now, just when they should have had many good years to look forward to.

'I agreed to come here today because I thought it would be rude not to,' Neil began. 'I haven't changed my mind, though. I can't manage without Viney at home, and that's all there is to it. In any case, as I've already explained to her, I don't hold with a lot of education for girls. It's wasted when they'll go and get married later on.'

Miss Thomas restrained herself with difficulty. She had met with a similar attitude in her own home and it was only after a great deal of fuss that she had been allowed to go to university. In her case her father's patronising remark had been: 'No man wants a wife who thinks she knows more than he does. It's not good for a marriage.'

'It would be different if it was just myself and the older lads, but you see, I have a little boy, just four years old, and someone has to be there for him.'

'Ah, yes, Aidan,' Miss Thomas murmured. A spoiled little horror, by what she'd heard, although perhaps she was doing him an injustice. As the petted latecomer, there might be nothing wrong with him that time wouldn't cure. Once he got to school he'd probably get the corners rubbed off in a hurry and, being out of the house all day, he wouldn't need his sister quite as much.

'Viney is too young to go off to nursing school this year in any case,' she told Neil. 'So why not leave making a final decision for the moment? You may find that things have changed a year from now.'

Neil's mouth twisted into a stubborn line. 'Perhaps you haven't heard what I've been saying, Miss Thomas.'

'Oh, but I have, Mr Lucas. You believe that Viney will marry eventually, which of course is quite likely. In that event, a nursing training will be a splendid preparation for marriage and motherhood, don't you think?'

'So will keeping house and minding Aidan!'

Miss Thomas was determined to salvage something from this interview. Not for nothing had she dealt over the years with insolent girls and resentful staff.

'Very well, Mr Lucas, I must abide by your decision. As her father, you must know what is best for Viney. However, could you find it in your heart to grant me one favour?'

'What's that, then?'

Ignoring the frown of suspicion which darkened his face, she hurried on. 'Please, can't she be allowed to sit her exams? She's worked so hard, and to obtain those qualifications would be the summit of her school career.' She hated herself for the pedantic language but she needed all the help she could get if she was to wring anything out of this situation for Viney. 'Your daughter is grieving over the loss of her mother, as you all are,' she went on. 'If you let her have this much, she will settle down and look after the home much more willingly, can't you see that?'

Neil hesitated, and she played her final card. 'She's a young girl who thought the whole world was about to open up to her. Instead, she's had a door slammed in her face. Do you want her to feel she's in prison now?'

The ploy worked. He knew what prison was. He understood the frustration, the anger, the despair which could come from having no control over one's own life. He didn't want that for his daughter.

'I don't see any harm in letting her sit the exams, then, so long as she understands it goes no farther,' he conceded.

When he had gone, Miss Thomas wiped her brow. At least she wouldn't have to resort to Plan B! If necessary she had been willing to look after Aidan herself while Viney, unbeknown to her father, tackled the eight exams she was meant to be sitting. The trouble she might have had to face afterwards was something else; the Board wouldn't have looked kindly on a headmistress who encouraged a pupil to do behind his back something which her father had expressly forbidden.

'Dad! Thank you! I promise I won't let you down.' Viney was jubilant when she heard the news. Good old Miss Thomas!

'Just as long as you don't let things slide on the home front,' he warned with a rare smile.

'Perhaps I'll get the boys to help a bit, at least until the exams are over,' she suggested, but he shook his head.

'The lads work hard all day and they cough up part of their money towards the housekeeping; that's right and proper. The rest is up to you.'

'Yes, Dad.' Having won the right to sit her exams, she felt it unwise to rock the boat. Besides, as Miss Thomas had pointed out, no nursing school would take her at her age, so she might as well spend her time in Lilac Lane as anywhere else.

'Ask your dad if I can come up there and spend a holiday with you,' Sybil wrote. 'I mean, maybe I shouldn't ask when everyone's grieving over Auntie Laura, but I could help you round the house until you get used to things. I can't get into nursing school yet either, so right now I'm free as a bird.'

'Let's wait till September,' Viney wrote back. 'With any luck Aidan will be in school then, if they take him, and we'll have some time to ourselves. Right now he's being an absolute pain! Remember little Sidney? He was an angel compared with my little brother. The trouble is, of course, that while we're all missing Mum dreadfully, he doesn't understand where she is. He keeps snivelling round the house, trying to find her, and that gets me blubbing, of course.'

'What do you mean, 'if they take him'?' Sybil wanted to know.

'Well, we love him to bits, of course,' Viney tried to explain, as the letters flew back and forth between London and Llanidris, 'but he's still not saying much, and he does fly into awful rages when he doesn't get his own way. Dad says I shouldn't give him his dinner until he can ask for it properly, or at least say please. Let him get hungry enough and he'll soon shape up, that's his answer to everything. But that seems cruel to me. Aidan's just a little boy who's lost his mummy. It's not time to 'get tough with him' as Mark thinks.'

★ ★ ★

The exam results came through and, with a dry mouth and a wobbly feeling in her stomach, Viney made her way to the school and searched the lists which were posted on the main door. To her relief she had passed all her subjects except the dreaded Chemistry. At least she had something to show for her years at the school. Miss Thomas had been right; having these qualifications did give her a warm glow which helped to reconcile her to the daily grind which was now hers.

'I failed Algebra,' Sybil mourned, 'but so what? Nurses don't need it. Mum was amazed at how well I did otherwise, and she wants me to stay on at school for A-levels. Can you imagine? Anyway, I told her to forget it because come September I'll be on my way to good old Llanidris. Is Mrs Jenkins next door still alive? And that nosy old Evans the Post? Is there anything you want me to bring you from London?'

163

It seemed that in no time at all it was September and Sybil was there, and the missing years had ebbed away and they were little girls again, rolling on the bed and telling secrets.

'Mark is gorgeous!' Sybil said. 'A real dish. Do you think he'd take me out if I asked him nicely?'

'You and every other girl in a ten-mile radius! Why don't you try Matt? He's always liked you.'

'Dear old Matt. He's a real pet, but Mark's the type I go for, dark and dangerous. No harm in trying, anyway.'

Sybil had grown into a most attractive girl. Her flaxen hair had darkened to a darker blonde, and her eyes sparkled. Viney had no idea that she herself was as pretty as they came, and she wished she had Sybil's looks.

Mark agreed at once when Sybil went into action. 'Take you to the hop, if you like,' he offered.

'What's a hop?'

'A young people's dance in the church hall. There's no band or anything, but they have a D.J. who plays all the latest records.'

'Fine with me. What do we wear, Viney?'

'Me? I won't be going. What would I do with Aidan?'

'Leave him with Uncle Neil, of course! You're not joined to him at the hip.'

'I don't like to ask,' Viney faltered, but Sybil pulled a face.

'Nonsense! If you won't say anything, I will!'

'Of course she can go,' Neil said, surprised. 'It's just that she's never asked before, that's all. Aidan can stay with me, can't you, boy?' Aidan nodded happily.

★ ★ ★

Viney stood against the wall, half hidden by a pillar. On the dance floor, Sybil was jiving madly, partnered by Mark. Her face was lit up in an expression of delight, and her blonde hair, twisted into two neat plaits, flew out behind her head as she moved. Many admiring glances came her way, but when other young men came forward to ask her for a dance, Mark told them she wasn't available.

Far from standing up for herself under this proprietary behaviour, Sybil seemed to enjoy the fact that she was clearly 'Mark's girl'.

Viney couldn't help feeling envious of her friend. If only she was more like her! Sybil was just over five feet four and had a city-girl air of confidence. Viney was five feet eight, which was the kiss of death as far as she was concerned; many of these local Welsh boys were shorter.

She had been bullied at school for being a foreigner, for having an odd name, and for being the tallest in her class. The most miserable day of her life had been when a well-meaning English teacher had praised an essay she had written, announcing to the class that Viney was 'head and shoulders above the rest of you.' Jeers had followed Viney for days after that.

Almost completely lacking in self-confidence, she was convinced that she was doomed to be a wallflower. Magazine articles told you how to behave when you went to a dance, and she had read several. You were supposed to smile and look animated; nobody would ask you to dance if you wore a sour expression.

Viney smiled bravely but nobody asked her to dance, which was a good thing really, she thought, because she didn't know how. She made several trips to the Ladies and still nobody came.

'Not dancing?'

'Oh, hi, Matt. Nobody's asked me yet.'

'I wanted to dance with Sybil,' he grumbled, 'but Mark's fending everyone off. I don't know what he thinks he's up to, monopolising her like that.'

'I bet lots of girls here would love to dance with you, Matt. Why don't you ask some of them?'

Matt grunted and she guessed that he must be suffering from the same kind of nerves as she was. It was too bad, really. He was nice looking in a quiet sort of way, and far more reliable than his younger brother.

'Let's dance the next one together, shall we?' she asked. Anything was better than standing here looking like lost sheep.

'Might as well, I suppose.' They sauntered on to the floor, falling over each other's feet as they tried to imitate the moves made by the more experienced dancers.

The evening finished with some slower tunes and to her amazement she was asked to dance the last dance with a boy who had spent most of the time at the refreshments table where lemonade and pop was for sale. The top of his head reached as high as her ear and she felt that everyone was looking at her, but at least she was saved from the disgrace of having no partner at all.

'See you home?' he mumbled, following tradition, but she managed to let him down lightly by saying that she had to walk back with her brothers, because her father was very strict. He plunged back into the crowd without asking if she would be there the following week.

There was no sign of Mark or Sybil when Viney joined Matt outside the hall, and the two walked back to Lilac Lane without saying much.

'Enjoy yourself, love?' Neil asked.

'Yes, thanks, Dad. Is Aidan all right?'

'Sound asleep. Where's your friend, then?'

'She was dancing with Mark all evening. I think she left with him.'

'He'll have taken her over to the garage to show her his car. It's his pride and joy; he shows it to all the girls.'

It was much later when the pair returned. Viney waited for a roar from her father, but nothing was said. At nineteen Mark was a grown man, and probably Neil didn't feel responsible for

169

the visitor from London as he might have for his own daughter.

'I had a wonderful time, didn't you?' This was Sybil, when the girls had retired to Viney's room with glasses of milk.

'You certainly seemed to enjoy yourself,' Viney responded. 'The lads were lining up to ask for a dance, and you turned them all down.'

'That was Mark's fault.' Sybil giggled. 'He was very masterful and fended them all off. I never thought that Llanidris could be such fun. Shall we go again next Saturday night?'

'You can if you like. I'd better stay home and let Dad go out. He likes to go down the Red Dragon for a pint and a chat with his mates.'

'Please yourself. Oh, Viney, I think I'm in love!'

Knowing Mark as she did, Viney hoped it was just a holiday romance. Sybil was in for a shock if she took him too seriously. A kiss or two in the moonlight was par for the course for him, with a different girl every week. She hoped that when Sybil returned to London she'd revert to thinking of Mark as just one of the boys she'd grown up with.

★　★　★

As things turned out, none of them made it to the hop the following week. Mark got into trouble at work and was in danger of losing his job, if not worse.

'What's your trouble, boy?' Neil demanded when they met at the tea table on Monday. 'You've got a face like thunder. Nothing wrong at work, is there?'

'Yes, there is, as a matter of fact. Old Price has only gone and accused me of stealing, that's all!'

'And that's not true, I suppose?'

'Dad!' he looked indignant.

'All right, steady on! What happened?'

'All Friday's money's gone out of the cash drawer. Mr Price usually goes to the bank on Fridays but he was called away from the office and I was told to lock up at the end of the day. Well, I did, and I dropped off the keys at his house on my way home, and that's all I know.'

Mark's face looked white and strained and Sybil patted his hand. 'Cheer up, Mark. We know you didn't do it.'

'Of course he didn't do it!' Neil snapped. 'And why would he lay the blame on you? You're not the only one working in his tuppenny-ha'penny garage!'

Mark scratched his ear. 'I was seen there on Saturday night. 'Hanging about', as the old man put it. I'm supposed to have left the door on the latch on Friday and nipped back the next night to do the dirty work.'

'That's a lie!' Sybil cried. 'We were there together, and I shall go and tell your boss so. Probably one of the other men stole the money while your back was turned, and it was gone before you even locked up. I mean, I'm sure you didn't go into the office to check the cash drawer, did you?'

'Of course not. It didn't occur to me that he would leave the money there. If he didn't have time to get to the bank he would take the cash-box home. That's what I thought.'

Mark couldn't be guilty — could he? Viney remembered all the times when, as a boy, he had taken things that didn't belong to him. Mostly it had been food or toys, yet probably that sort of thing happened in most families. Of course, there was also that time when he'd taken a pot of jam from the shop. Poor Mum, she'd been beside herself on that occasion!

But Mark was grown up now and surely knew better. But then Viney recalled all the times when he'd grumbled about not having enough money to buy parts for his car, or to take a girl to the cinema . . .

She chided herself for being horrid. Where was her family loyalty?

True to her word, Sybil braved Mr Price in his den and insisted that there was no way Mark could have entered the office on Saturday.

'And you needn't suggest that I was his accomplice, either,' she announced, her eyes flashing, 'because I wasn't. I give you my word of honour!'

Mr Price gave some thought to this before nodding wryly. 'I believe you, young miss, but that still doesn't help me catch the culprit, or get my money back!'

'Then dock all their pay,' she suggested. 'That way, you'll get your money back, and the innocent ones will lean on the guilty party until he coughs up!'

# Love Is In the Air

Once again Sybil was being seen off at the station, but this time Viney was the only member of the family there. Every once in a while Sybil would peer anxiously in the direction of the station yard and Viney knew she was hoping for Mark to appear, but he didn't.

Viney wiped away a tear, remembering how they had come here with poor Mum, when Sybil had gone back to London after the war.

'Promise me you'll write and tell me how everyone is,' Sybil begged.

'Of course. And you let me know every last thing that happens when you start at St Martha's. Oh, I wish I was going with you!'

Viney felt flat as she went home. There was nothing much to look forward to now until Christmas.

As things turned out, however, there

were two events which shook up the placid round of her days. Remarkably, Aidan began to talk, and Mark left home.

Viney had feared for Aidan when he started at the Llanidris school, knowing from experience how cruel children can be to anyone who's a bit different. There was certain to be some name-calling when they discovered that he didn't talk. However, as Dr Foy had long ago suspected, it was a case of wouldn't rather than couldn't, for on his second day in Standard One the child began to spill out a few words, hesitantly at first but gradually improving until the flow increased.

'I always knew there was nothing wrong,' Neil observed with satisfaction. 'If you women hadn't spoiled him so much he'd have spoken up long since.'

'That's not fair, Dad!' Viney cried. 'I've spent hours trying to make him say something, but he'd only laugh and wriggle off my lap.'

'What's it matter, love? He's chattering away now, all right.'

'He's still refusing to say please and thank you, though,' Viney muttered, but her father only laughed, saying, 'Boys will be boys. You mustn't turn him into a namby pamby, love.'

This made Viney very cross. Dad couldn't have it both ways. It was her fault that Aidan hadn't talked before and now she wasn't supposed to teach him any manners!

As promised, Sybil did write. Evans the Post pushed several envelopes through the letter-box which Viney recognised as coming from her friend. Nobody else used scented paper and green ink. Two were addressed to Mark, but he took them from Viney with a grunt and later she found them in the bin, unopened. Clicking her tongue she fed the letters into the fire, not wanting the dustmen to see them when they made their weekly rounds.

'Why doesn't Mark answer my letters?' Sybil pleaded, her looped writing spread all over the page. 'Tell me what's going on with him, Viney. Did they ever find out who stole the money?'

'Yes, they did,' Viney wrote back. 'There was a very unpleasant atmosphere at the garage for days, or so Mark told us. Then Mrs Vernon — that's Mr Price's married daughter — turned up with her teenaged daughter, practically dragging the girl by the ear. Apparently she had been in to visit her grandfather on the day the money had gone missing and had helped herself while his back was turned.'

Viney could see it all in her mind's eye. When cleaning out her daughter's room Mrs Vernon had discovered a pile of rock and roll records, far too many to have been purchased with Nancy's pocket money. Challenged, the girl had said she'd borrowed them from a friend, but when a new cap-sleeved blouse and a lacy black bra had also come to light, there was no denying that something was going on.

'Where did you get all this money, my girl?' Mrs Vernon, a pillar of the Wesleyan chapel, had been terrible in her wrath.

'Grandpa gave it to me — for my birthday, he said,' Nancy had insisted.

'Your birthday isn't until February!'

'I expect he forgot. You know what his memory's like these days.'

'Then you should have reminded him. I don't believe a word of this, Nancy Vernon. Get your coat on. We're going down the garage to hear what he has to say.'

Making tea in the cubby-hole next to the office, Mark had heard the raised voices and put his ear to the door.

'To think that any daughter of mine could be a liar and a thief . . . ' That had been Mrs Vernon.

'And to think that one of my best men stands falsely accused!' had come old Price's voice. 'There's wicked you are, Nancy Vernon. You've broken your poor mother's heart, I know!'

Mark had moved away from the door. So he was one of old Price's best men, was he? He'd grinned, wondering if he could make the old chap stump up a raise when he came to apologise.

Nancy, pushed forward, had muttered an unconvincing 'Sorry' to Mark, who had glared at his boss.

'That's all very well, Mr Price, but that's no help to me, is it? Everyone in Llanidris thinks I'm a thief, and you know how mud sticks.'

'They'll know different now, Lucas, although it cuts me to the quick to have to tell people that my own grandchild would steal from me, or from anyone else, for that matter. So you can carry on as before, and we'll say no more about it.'

'That's all very well for him to say,' Mark had grumbled to his father that night. 'Here's me, innocent as a new-born lamb, and all he can say is we'll go on as before! Not a word about compensation. And you can say what you like, Dad, nobody's going to believe me over that little madam with her big blue eyes!'

'Her mother believes you,' Neil had reminded him, but Mark had still harboured a sense of grievance.

A month later he arrived home and announced that he was leaving.

'Leaving!' His father was shocked. 'Where are you planning to go?'

'Cardiff. I've got a job in a garage there. It pays twice as much as I get at Price's and I'll see a bit of life in the city. A different type of car to work on, too, I shouldn't wonder.'

'Well, this is a surprise, son! I had no idea you were thinking of leaving us.'

'Huh! After what happened over that money, I don't feel like staying on. Price was quite willing to believe I'm a thief, and that hurt, Dad. For two pins I'd have walked out there and then, but I thought it best to wait until I landed another job.'

So Mark packed his belongings into his old car and set off for the bright lights. Sybil begged Viney to pass on his new address, which Viney did, while knowing that Mark had no intention of replying.

Now that Aidan was talking, it was discovered that he had a very nice little soprano voice.

'Now he's learning all sorts of songs at school and Mr Smart is talking about roping him in as a soloist in the church choir!' Viney told Matt.

'All the old ladies will love him,' Matt declared. 'Imagine our Aidan all dolled up in a white surplice, looking like a little angel!'

John, who was a keen Scout, did his part by teaching his little brother all the campfire songs he knew.

Viney could only be glad that Aidan had found his feet at last. Now that he was at school all day, and often out playing with his new friends at the weekends, she had more time to herself, and when she ran across an old schoolfriend, Ceridwen, life became more bearable. The pair started playing tennis together at the park on Saturday mornings, and at other times they walked beside the river, telling each other their hopes and dreams.

It was through Ceridwen that Viney met George Blaney, who was to become the love of her life. Ceridwen worked at the Daffodil Laundry, although not in the steam-filled work-rooms, as she was quick to tell anyone who asked, but in the office, where she did typing and filing.

'There's a smashing new chap doing deliveries,' she told Viney. 'Not that he's my type, mind. I've still got hopes for Dai Williams, if I can wrest him away from that girlfriend of his. George Blaney, his name is. He's not from round here so he doesn't know anybody yet. I told him about you, and he wants to meet you.'

'You didn't!'

'What's wrong with that? You don't have a boyfriend, do you? If I fix you up with George you can at least go out with him once. Take him to the hop or something. If it doesn't work out, what have you lost?'

Viney wasn't convinced. 'How tall is he? I'm not going out with someone who only comes up to my elbows.'

'He's five-ten. I asked him. So how about it?'

'Oh, all right, I'll give it a go.'

So Viney went to the pictures with George and she had to admit she was favourably impressed. He wasn't exactly handsome but he had a pleasant face and his brown hair was thick and nicely cut. He didn't talk about himself much but answered her questions in good-humoured fashion, and he seemed interested in all she had to say.

When he asked her to go out for a walk after church on Sunday she was hesitant at first, explaining that if her father wanted to go out she would have Aidan on her hands. But George wasn't put off.

'I don't mind. We can take him with us — the little brother, I mean, not your dad!'

These outings were a source of great

pleasure to Viney, and she soon realised that she was falling in love for the first time.

'What made you think of working for the Daffodil?' she asked. In the way of all lovers since the beginning of time she wanted to know everything there was to know about the man of her choice.

'I was at a loose end after finishing my National Service and it so happened that one of my mates in the Air Force is from Llanidris. He heard about the job and I thought it would be a start while I look around for something else. This job's all right, but the pay isn't wonderful, and I want to do more with my life than delivering bags of sheets!'

'I know what you mean,' she said with feeling. 'I always wanted to be a nurse, but it hasn't worked out.'

'What happened? Weren't your O-levels good enough?' he asked.

She found herself telling him all about her mum's death, and how she'd had to leave school to keep house for her father and the boys.

'Never mind. I expect you'll get married some day, and they don't let married women work as nurses, do they? Not in hospital, anyway.'

Viney felt a warm glow. Was he suggesting that the pair of them might get married some day?

If Viney was happy with the way things were between her and George, she was definitely worried about Aidan. He seemed bright enough in some ways, yet school work seemed another matter. Not everyone was academic, of course, and he was still very young, but surely he should be learning more now that he'd been at school for all these months?

She tried to encourage him by pointing out simple words in the story books she read to him at bedtime. He would repeat these when she said them, but when she returned later to the same word on the printed page he seemed to have no idea. Perhaps she wasn't going about it in the right way, not being a teacher herself.

Then she tried some simple arithmetic. 'What's one and one, Aidan?'

'One and one!' he said brightly, stubbornly refusing to say 'two' when prompted. She had better luck when she produced some of John's old toy soldiers to use as counters, although she still wasn't sure that anything had really sunk in.

Matters came to a head one Monday morning when she was getting ready to start the weekly wash. Carefully going through everyone's pockets to be sure they were empty, she came across a crumpled paper in Aidan's shorts. It was a letter from his teacher, asking their father to attend a meeting at the school.

'What on earth for?' Neil wondered, when he heard about this. 'It's probably about some sort of fund-raising stunt. You'd better go, Viney. She'll have a long wait if she expects me to make fairy cakes.'

Viney was in the habit of going to the

school to meet Aidan after class, so she turned up at three-thirty, making her way through the little knot of mothers who were there for the same reason. She found her brother in the cloakroom, earnestly searching for his cap.

'Here it is, Ade. Look at the name tag. See? It says A.Lucas.'

Grinning, he snatched it from her and was about to run off when she held him back and told him to wait outside the classroom door. Then, with her heart in her mouth, she knocked and went in.

Miss Grant was a pleasant young woman, probably in her late twenties, Viney thought. She frowned when Viney introduced herself.

'I'm afraid Aidan is having a bit of trouble settling down. That's why I wrote to Mr Lucas. I gather he wasn't able to come today?'

'Er, no. He thought it was something to do with the school fete, and as I've brought Aidan up since our mother died, I . . . '

'Quite. Well, as I say, he's proved to be rather disruptive in class, to the point where I find it hard to keep order. I was wondering if you could shed any light on why this might be. Is everything all right at home, for instance?'

'Oh, yes. But I've been a bit worried because he doesn't seem to be learning as quickly as we expected.'

'That's hardly surprising when he can't seem to buckle down. Standard One is a child's first introduction to school routine, and it takes some longer than others to adjust. In Aidan's case, he just doesn't pay attention, but he certainly likes to be the centre of attention.'

'What does that mean, exactly?'

'Acting the clown, giving ridiculous answers, even getting out of his seat sometimes and roaming about.'

Viney could understand that this made things difficult for the teacher, but she wondered what she was expected to do about it. She tried to explain about Aidan's lack of speech, saying that possibly his progress was delayed in other ways as well.

'Has he been seen by a doctor, Miss Lucas?'

'You mean for his vaccinations and so on?'

'No, I mean has he been assessed to see if he suffers from a disability of any sort?'

Viney was taken aback. 'I think Mum took him to our doctor when he wasn't starting to talk, but I don't know what happened after that.'

'Then it might be time to take him back again, don't you think?' Miss Grant suggested.

'You'd better take him up to the surgery then,' Neil grunted when given this news. 'A lot of silly nonsense, I call it. It's not our problem if the woman can't keep order. In my day, we got rapped over the knuckles with a book if we played up. Still, you go and see what old Foy has to say this time, then at least you can tell the teacher we've done our best.'

★ ★ ★

Viney ushered Aidan into the doctor's surgery, stopping short when she saw that it wasn't old Dr Foy who was sitting there, but a much younger man.

'I'm Dr Russell, Dr Foy's locum,' he explained. 'Dr Foy is away on holiday. Now, what can I do for this young man?'

Viney explained, and then the doctor asked Aidan a few simple questions — did he play football, did he like animals, and so on.

'Nothing wrong with his speech now!' He laughed. 'Does he know his letters, Miss Lucas?'

'That's part of the problem, Doctor. He doesn't seem to be learning much of anything, although Llanidris is a good school. I went there myself at his age.'

'Not to worry. I've got another chart

with pictures on it. You come and sit here, young man, and we'll have a look, shall we?'

When he had finished his examination he turned to Viney with a sigh. 'No wonder he's learning nothing. This child can't see the blackboard! He needs spectacles, that's all. Has nobody ever thought of that?'

\* \* \*

Over the next three years dozens of letters flew back and forth between Viney and Sybil. Sybil had been accepted into St Martha's and at first she said little about it.

'I don't want to hurt your feelings, Viney,' she wrote. 'If things had been different you'd have been sharing this with me so I feel really awkward telling you much.'

'You needn't worry about me,' Viney replied. 'Yes, there was a time when it would have upset me, but not any more. Now I have George I think perhaps it was meant to be. I'm happier than I've ever been in my life, Sybil, and I do hope you feel the same.'

'I don't know about that,' Sybil wrote. 'Being a trainee nurse is like being a parlourmaid. It's clean this, wash that, oil the wheels on that trolley, empty that bedpan. They have a thing called damp dusting where you have to mop all the furniture and window-sills with a damp cloth every day.'

'At least the uniform is glamorous,' Viney responded. 'I loved that photo you sent me, showing you in your cap.'

'Glamorous my foot! You should see the length of the uniform dresses we have to wear. It's almost a sin to show your ankles in this place.'

Sybil continued to moan, but Viney suspected she was loving it all.

'But never mind me, Viney. How's Aidan getting on these days? Is he more settled at school?'

Aidan was indeed doing better, although mental arithmetic posed problems for him.

'He doesn't stop to think,' Miss Grant complained when Viney turned up to hear the worst on parents' night. 'You ask him a question and he'll fire off three or four different answers, one after the other, I suppose in the hope that one will be the correct one. In a way it might have been better if your doctor had prescribed something to calm him down. I wish you'd speak to your father about it.'

'Stuff and nonsense!' Neil said. 'Tell her to leave the boy alone. Not everybody is a genius at maths; I wasn't myself if it comes to that. I don't believe in giving pills to a child for no reason. I'm just thankful he's well and happy, that's all.'

Viney wished she could speak to young Dr Russell again, to ask his opinion, but as soon as he had finished filling in during Dr Foy's absence he had gone back to where he had come from, wherever that might be.

Meanwhile, Aidan went on his merry way, and when he turned out to be quite a good reader she had to admit that perhaps her dad had been right all along. Then, too, the child seemed endowed with a good memory, for he was always spouting off bits of Welsh history which he had learned at school.

George was beginning to get restless. 'Any fool can drive a van,' he told Viney. 'I'm fed up with the Daffodil Laundry. I'm thinking of applying for a job at the bakery. At least I'd have the horse to talk to on my rounds.'

'I know what he should do,' Ceridwen told Viney when she heard about this. 'Tell him to go and see Mr Price.'

'Mr Price? You mean where our Mark used to work?'

'Yes. My brother's a mechanic, too, and he started work there recently. The thing is, Mr Price has bought the old bicycle shop next door to the garage, and he's going to turn it into a car showroom. Since the war a lot of ordinary people have been treating themselves to a car and he says he wants to get in on the action.'

'He won't get many cars inside the old bike shed,' Viney objected, but her friend brushed off this suggestion.

'Cadoc says the building's going to be pulled down and something bigger put up in its place. And there's going to be a forecourt where other vehicles can be displayed.'

Viney passed the news on to George, although she didn't have much hope of his getting the job.

He whistled. 'I say, that's a good idea! I think I'll call round and see Mr Price this evening.'

'There's no job to go to until the place is built.'

'Of course not, but once the news gets out there'll be a queue a mile long. I'll get in first, before anyone else has the chance.'

'What are you going to say when he asks you what you know about cars? You've never seen the inside of a car, let alone put one to rights.'

'My dear girl, I'll be a salesman, not a mechanic! And what do you think I do with all those car magazines I buy?'

'You gloat over them, don't you, dreaming of the day when you'll be able to afford a car of your own!'

'Yes, I do, but I know all about the most popular makes, their different features, and what they cost to buy, new. And that's what I shall tell Mr Price. I'll suggest he should also carry some second-hand models, which his mechanics can put in good repair before they go on sale. Not everyone can afford a brand-new vehicle, even now that people can buy things on the Never Never.'

The system of credit which had come into popularity since the war enabled many people to furnish their homes or to buy other luxuries for which they couldn't find ready cash. The name came from the saying that customers would never never finish paying for these items because of the high interest rates attached to the scheme. The beauty of the credit system, as far as the seller was concerned, was that if buyers failed to keep up the payments the items could be repossessed.

Mr Price was quite taken with George, seeing in him a personable young man with a good work record. He was twenty-four years old, which in Mr Price's eyes meant that he would soon be settling down to marriage and a family, and would thus be a reliable employee.

'Mind you, he didn't want to pay me much,' George reported back to Viney. 'I had to haggle before he'd even go as high as my current wage. But as I said, there's no point in my leaving the laundry only to get less money.'

'So what did he say to that?'

'Well, in the end he agreed to pay me the same as I'm getting now, but with commission added on if I sell any cars. When I sell cars,' he added firmly.

'So I suppose you'll be getting your own car soon then. Staff discount and all that.'

'Oh, no, I shan't be doing that. I have plans for the future, which means I'll be putting every penny I can in the bank. I should do quite well since I don't have many expenses other than the board and lodging I pay my landlady.'

Viney had no idea what those plans were, but she hoped they included her. She had already started to fill her bottom drawer with bits and pieces, and now she took a leaf out of George's book and began putting a bit of money into her post office savings account whenever she could. Dad gave her a some pocket money each week, and when it came to Christmas or her birthday he was quite generous.

\* \* \*

John passed his O-levels with flying colours and announced his intention of staying on at the grammar school to do A-levels in Biology, Chemistry and Physics.

'I'm going to be a doctor some day,' he told Viney, his eyes shining.

'I wanted to be a nurse once,' she

said. 'It's good to be able to help people when they need it, John.'

'I know you did, but you had to give up the idea when Mum died and you were needed here. We needed help and you gave it to us, Viney. That's as good as going to nurse a lot of people we don't even know.'

Viney was surprised and touched. It was the first time any of the family had thought of thanking her for her sacrifice and the sentiment was something of a miracle coming from a teenaged boy!

'It's what anybody would have done,' she murmured and they smiled at each other for a long moment before Aidan bounced in, wanting to know if she had made any cake.

'Yes, I made a chocolate sponge, as it happens. But I'm saving it for tomorrow when George is coming to tea. You'll get your share then.'

He groaned, and his eyes went to the cake tin, but Viney told him that if he knew what was good for him he'd keep his hands off the sponge, or she'd have his guts for garters.

★　★　★

'I'm engaged!' Sybil wrote, her large green lettering sprawling across the page. 'What do you think of that?'

'Who to?' Viney wrote back, aware as she did so that her English teacher would have scolded her for using bad grammar. But 'To whom' sounded too fancy between friends, or so she had always thought.

Sybil's reply came straight back. 'Idiot! It's Derek, of course! Haven't we been going out for ages? Don't I mention him in every other sentence? Of course, we can't get married yet. I want to finish my training first, because it seems such a waste if I give up now. And we have to save up, which isn't easy on a nurse's salary, even though I'm a third-year now with great responsibilities!'

'Tell me again what it is that Derek

does,' Viney responded. 'I know it's something to do with the hospital but he isn't a doctor, is he?'

'Not in that sense, although he has a doctoral degree. He does very important medical research at St Martha's. Just think, Viney, some day I may be the wife of a Nobel Prize-winner. Generations to come may bless the name of Derek Parker.'

'I notice that you've had another letter from your friend,' Neil observed. 'She churns them out like nobody's business. They can't be very busy at that hospital of hers if she has all this spare time.'

'She's on nights, Dad. She wrote this one at three o'clock in the morning. They were having a quiet night and she had to do something to keep herself awake. She'd be in real trouble if Night Sister popped in and found her fast asleep at the desk!'

'What does she have to say for herself, anyway? She must be nearing the end of her training now.'

Viney nodded. 'Just a few more months. She's engaged to be married, by the way. They haven't set the date yet, but I expect it'll be soon after she graduates.'

'There, isn't that just what I've said all along?' Neil said, folding his newspaper neatly. 'They've spent three years training the girl, and now she'll be throwing it all up and the hospital won't reap the benefit. And don't give me that stuff about nursing being a useful preparation for marriage, either. A woman can learn those skills on the job. Your mother did, and so did mine.'

This was an old argument and Viney didn't rise to the bait. Sybil had already addressed that question in any case, writing: 'They get three years' hard grind out of us while we're training, working up to twelve hours a day, and all we get is a few shillings a week pocket money. If hospitals had to pay their nurses what they really deserve, they'd never be able to afford them.'

As Viney knew, apart from one staff nurse and a sister, all the nurses on each ward were girls at various stages of their training. On the other side of the coin was the fact that students didn't have to pay for their excellent training so the system was one of mutual benefit.

That last letter had held other exciting news for Viney.

'She wants me to be her bridesmaid when the time comes, Dad. She says I'm the next best thing she has to a sister.'

'And quite right, too, after all your mother did for her during the war.'

'What does Sybil have to say for herself, then?' Matt wanted to know when he came in and saw the letter propped up on the sideboard.

'She's getting married, though not just yet, and I'm to be her bridesmaid.'

He looked so woebegone that Viney almost laughed.

'Don't tell me you're still carrying a torch for her, Matt!'

'I think I've loved her for as long as I can remember.'

'Puppy love, that was. Or brotherly love, if you prefer. Nobody really has lasting feelings at that age.'

He sighed. 'I did, and when she came to visit us three years ago, I felt more strongly about her than ever. For two pins I'd have proposed to her then, but I let the opportunity slip, and now it's too late.'

Viney stared at him. 'Why on earth didn't you speak up at the time?'

'And how was I supposed to do that, when Mark wouldn't let me get a look-in? And you must admit that she was besotted with him then. If I'd said anything she'd have laughed in my face.'

'Oh, I doubt if she'd have done that,' Viney murmured, but it was true that Sybil had fancied Mark and indeed it had taken her a long time to forget him. It was a good thing that she had Derek now. But first love was painful, and now it appeared that Matt's first love was Sybil. It was to be hoped that he would meet somebody new and fall in love in a more mature way.

He seemed to have accepted the situation because instead of moping around the house as Viney had feared, he asked a very nice girl named Brenda to go out with him, and from that day on they seemed to be inseparable. Perhaps the worst was over.

\* \* \*

'Guess what?' Viney exclaimed when she saw George. 'My best friend, Sybil, has just got engaged.'

'I thought Ceridwen was your best friend.'

'Well, she is, I suppose, here in Llanidris, but I'm talking about the girl who stayed with us during the war.'

'Oh, her. I forgot her name, that's all. So she's getting married? I suppose you'll be looking forward to getting married next,' he said.

'Oh, I expect I'll take the plunge some day.' She laughed 'That's if anybody asks me.'

'Oh, somebody will ask you, all right,' he replied, looking very serious. 'I was going to wait until your birthday and do the thing properly, with wine and a romantic setting somewhere, but now the subject's come up, I may as well test the water. Viney, I've loved you for a long time, and I think we could make a go of it. Will you marry me?'

'Oh, George, I love you too, and of course I'll marry you!' Time stood still as they stood clasped in each other's arms, barely aware of their surroundings.

George was first to disengage himself. 'Sorry, love. The village street is no place for a proposal, is it? Never mind, we'll do it all again later on. I'm afraid it's going to be a long while before we can actually set the date though. I haven't sold as many cars as I'd hoped, and I'm in no position to keep a wife, let alone start a family.'

In a daze of happiness, Viney didn't care that her proposal had taken place in the middle of nowhere. Her girlish fantasies of having a lover declare himself in a rose-covered bower, or drifting downstream in a punt, were just that, romantic dreams. It was enough to know that she was loved, and that she would be spending the rest of her life with George.

Her thoughts flew ahead to the future. She would be Mrs George Blaney. She had to admit that Viney Blaney sounded a bit awkward. Perhaps she would revert to Lavinia when signing things. Lavinia Blaney wasn't half bad.

George was trying to get her attention. 'I said, I'll ring my parents tonight and tell them the good news. Will you tell your father?'

'Of course. I hope he'll be pleased.'

Neil took the news with a smile. 'That's good, love. George seems like a nice chap. Of course, you're a bit young yet, aren't you?'

'Dad! I'm twenty! We're going to have to wait, though. George doesn't have much saved up. The car business hasn't really got going yet, or not as well as he'd hoped.'

'Time for him to look around for other work, then. Tell him to contact Mark. There might be better pickings in Cardiff.'

'Oh, I wouldn't want him to move there. When would I ever see him?'

'It's either one thing or the other, love. Stay here in poverty or go where there may be more opportunities. It's worth making a few sacrifices if it helps in the end.'

Viney smiled. 'Perhaps. I'm just going up to put flowers on Mum's grave now.'

'And tell her about George, I suppose. Give her my best love, Viney.'

* * *

'Lucky you!' Ceridwen enthused. 'When are you getting the ring?' 'On my twenty-first birthday, George says. I'm so excited I can hardly believe it's true.'

'Ooh, I wish I was you! I can't wait to get away from home. Mam's such a

209

fuss-post. Always wanting to know where I'm going and when I'm going to be back, and then having a fit if I'm five minutes late!'

'You don't have to be married to leave home, not these days. Why don't you get a flat of your own?'

'On what they pay me at the Daffodil? That's a joke, that is.'

'So get another girl to share the cost.'

Ceridwen's eyes lit up. 'I say, do you fancy it?'

'Oh, sorry, I didn't mean me. No, I've got to save all I can or we'll be old and grey before we finally tie the knot. Anyway, you'll be next — getting engaged, I mean. Can't you bring Roger to the point?'

'Him? No, he's OK to hang around with but as a marriage prospect he's a dead loss. Do you think I want to spend my entire life shivering on a wet field while he plays rugby with his mates? I want someone who'll pay attention to me. I'm getting properly fed-up playing second fiddle to a bunch of men in short trousers. I'm thinking of chucking him, see?'

'Half a loaf is better than no bread, as they say.'

'I don't know about bread, but rumour has it that Dai Williams is available again. That Myfanwy Pritchard has given him the elbow. If I move fast I might get him to go out with me. What do you think?'

'It's worth a try,' Viney grinned.

Now, if only Matt's problems could be solved so easily, everything in the garden would be lovely, she thought. He was going through the motions with Brenda but unless something changed in a hurry, there didn't seem to be a future in it.

One way and another, though, everyone in Viney's world seemed to be pairing off and she was in a whirl of happiness at being part of it.

This joyful state of affairs lasted for precisely two months, and then the sky fell in.

'I've heard from my father,' George said. 'He wants to see me about something, so he's coming to Cardiff and I'm to meet him there.'

'Why Cardiff?'

'Because there's nowhere for him to stay in Llanidris. My bedsit's barely big enough for me, never mind Dad as well. But listen, Viney, why don't you come too? It's a nice ride by train and you'd enjoy the outing. We'll have a nice meal with Dad at his hotel and perhaps take in a film as well. He'd love to meet you. He can take back a report to Mum. She's dying to know all about her prospective daughter-in-law.'

'That sounds lovely, George. I'll have to see if Dad can manage without me, though, before I give you an answer.'

'Phooey! Of course he can manage! Leave him a pork pie and salad or something.'

'It's Aidan I'm worried about.'

'Ask Mrs Jenkins if she'll see to him. I bet she's an old romantic at heart. Tell her that Dad has come to inspect you, to see if you're good enough to join the Blaneys!'

So, dressed in her Sunday best, Viney met Rod Blaney and took an instant liking to him. He was probably in his early fifties but looked younger, and was very much like his son, both in features and colouring.

Viney was impressed by the hotel dining-room with its linen, sparkling silverware and crystal glasses.

'I say, Dad, this is going to cost you something, isn't it?' George hissed after studying the menu.

'It's not every day we have something like this to celebrate.' Rod beamed. 'Your mother and I talked it over and we decided that just for once money should be no object. Now, shall we start with the soup, or go straight to the main course?'

Pleased and flattered by this, Viney decided that she was going to enjoy being part of the Blaney family if they were so welcoming and kindly.

It wasn't until they had finished dessert and were lingering over coffee that she realised they might have been talking at cross purposes.

'Shall we take our coffee into the lounge?' George's father suggested. 'Then I can say what I've come to say in comfort.'

Couches and deep armchairs were placed in 'conversation settings' around small tables, and Rod Blaney led the way to one of these arrangements before starting to talk.

'Here's the thing. We've decided to emigrate, George. We're all going to Australia.'

George leaned forward, looking interested. 'Who's we, Dad?'

'Why, all of us. Me, your mother, and the rest of the family.'

'George didn't tell me you were thinking of leaving Britain, Mr Blaney. Have you been thinking about it for long?' Viney felt slightly out of her depth but was determined to keep her end up in the conversation. She didn't want her father-in-law to think she was a country mouse who didn't fit in.

'Well, you know, things haven't been the same since the war, what with rationing and all that, and I've come to the conclusion that the youngsters will have more opportunities over there. Not only that, but my wife hasn't been well for some time and I believe the climate will be better for her in Australia; all that sunshine, you see? Oh, she's not ill exactly,' he said, turning to George, who was looking worried. 'I know she can pass the necessary medicals, but our damp weather doesn't do her a lot of good. Just take a look at this!'

He fumbled in his jacket pocket and brought out some brochures. They contained brilliantly-coloured photos of people frolicking on sandy beaches under sunny skies and bronzed youngsters walking to school in their shirt sleeves, the picture of health.

'But how can you afford to take all the family there, Dad?' George asked. 'The fares must be pretty steep.'

'That's the beauty of it, son. Australia wants new settlers. We can get passages for just ten pounds a head.'

'Phew! It's certainly something to think about, but I shouldn't rush into anything until you know more about it.'

Rod Blaney shook his head. 'On these terms there's sure to be a rush and we should get started while the going's good. Who knows how long they'll keep an offer like this open. We don't want to miss out. The fact is, George, we've already applied, and we want you to come with us.'

George didn't answer at once, but Viney could tell that he was intrigued. 'What about us?' she wanted to shout but she managed to keep quiet. The last thing she wanted was to make a scene.

'Well, boy, I can see you want some time to think about it, but don't leave it too long, will you?'

'I won't, Dad. I'll let you know in a

day or two, all right?'

The magic of the day had disappeared as far as Viney was concerned. All the way home in the train George seemed preoccupied and she shrank into the corner seat, not wanting to break in on his mood. This silence lasted until they got off the train at the local station.

'Let's not wait for the bus, shall we?' he said then. 'I feel like a walk. Can you manage all right in those heels?'

'I daresay I can,' she muttered, thinking that a few blisters would be a small price to pay if only she could get him on his own to find out what was going through his mind.

At last he started to speak. 'This came as a shock to me, as you can well imagine. But now I've had time to mull it over, I think it's a great idea. I mean, what is there here for people like us?'

'I hope you're not one of those people who say that Britain's finished,' Viney snapped. 'Any country is what you make it. We managed to stick it out during the war and things are getting better all the time now.'

He seemed not to have heard her. 'You know, it's not at all a bad idea. My job is taking me nowhere, and at the rate I'm going we won't be able to get married until I'm thirty-five! Australia may be just what I need. New horizons, a great new job of some sort, and all those spectacular beaches to relax on. And if I go, I shan't have to say goodbye to my family. It all makes sense, Viney.'

By now they had reached Lilac Lane. George gave her a peck on the cheek. 'I don't think I'll come in. I'm tired out after all that. See you tomorrow, OK?'

And off he strode, leaving Viney standing at her gate, with her mind in a whirl.

# Thousands of Miles Apart

They were standing under a sycamore tree in a fine drizzle of rain. George pulled Viney round to face him and planted a light kiss on her forehead.

'Why so glum? You've hardly said a word all evening.'

'Is that surprising?'

'I don't know what you mean. Have I done something to offend you?'

'Oh, no, nothing at all. First you ask me to marry you and then a few months later you decide to swan off to the other side of the world. And where does that leave me?'

'So that's what this is about. Give me a break, Viney. It was a shock to me when I found out that my parents and the rest of the family are emigrating. It took me a while to get my mind round that.'

'But can you deny that you're

planning to go with them?'

'Not exactly. It's true I've thought it over but I haven't made a final decision yet. Naturally I wanted to talk it over with you first.'

'That's big of you!'

'Come on, love. Going to Australia has plenty to recommend it. Think of it, Viney — we could be spending next Christmas on a beach, feeling sorry for all those pour souls left behind in foggy old Britain!'

'You said 'we'. Do you mean you want me to come, too?'

'What did you think I had in mind? We're engaged, aren't we? We'll just bring our wedding forward and go out as a married couple.'

Viney's jaw dropped. Australia! Did she really want to go twelve thousand miles away from everything and everybody she loved? Yet she knew she would go to the moon if it meant being with the man she loved. And as for leaving home . . . why, that was what women did when they got married. You followed where your husband led.

'I'll need time to think,' she warned. 'And I'll have to speak to Dad. I'll need permission if I want to marry you before I'm twenty-one.'

'Of course. Don't leave it too long, though. There's plenty of paperwork and red tape to get through. And then there's the wedding itself. Are you keen on a big do at All Saints' church or will the registry office suit you?'

'I don't know. I haven't thought. As I said, I need time!'

'You will have a word with your father though, won't you?'

'Yes, yes. Now let's change the subject, shall we? I've got rain trickling down my neck and a cramp in my leg. We'd better move on.'

★   ★   ★

'Can I have a word, Dad?'

Viney hoped she'd picked the right moment for a heart-to-heart. Matt was out somewhere and John was frowning over his homework at the kitchen table. Aidan was upstairs asleep. At least, she hoped he was. It was his habit to come wandering down at inconvenient moments, and she wanted her father's full attention.

Neil put his paper down reluctantly. 'Yes, what is it?'

Viney took a deep breath. 'I've been talking to George, Dad, and we'd like to bring our wedding forward.' One shock at a time, she thought. That's the way to do it.

'Lavinia Lucas! Don't tell me there's some pressing reason for this! I never would have believed that any daughter of mine . . .'

'No, no, Dad, it's not what you're thinking, honestly!' Viney was red-faced with embarrassment. 'But something has come up and we'd like to get married sooner.'

He scratched his head. 'I suppose a few months either way won't make much difference. You bring me whatever papers I need to sign.'

'Thanks, Dad! I knew I could count on you.'

'So what are your plans? I know George just has that bedsit and you can't start your married life in that. He could come here, I suppose. Ask Matt if he'll take your room and the pair of you can have the annexe.'

'That won't be necessary, Dad. The Blaneys are emigrating to Australia and George wants me to marry him before we leave.'

He looked aghast. 'Leave? *Australia?* This is the first I've heard about Australia! I wouldn't have said I'd sign if I'd known that.'

'But, Dad, you knew I'd be leaving home when I got married. It's just happening a bit sooner than we expected, that's all, and I'll be going a bit farther.'

Neil's face wore the shuttered look that Viney had come to know only too well.

'You have a responsibility to Aidan, Viney. Either George comes here, or you take Aidan with you when you move out. It's as simple as that.'

Viney pointed out that Aidan wasn't her child, but his. She had looked after him ever since mother died, but now it was time for her to move on.

It cut no ice with Neil. 'I'm sorry, but that's not possible. The boy's doing well these days but he's still too young to manage on his own. I'm off to work before he gets up in the morning, and then he's back home before I knock off. He could get into any sort of mischief. Do you want me to be reported to the child protection people?'

'I'm sure we could arrange something for him, Dad. John could see him off to school in the morning, and perhaps he could go home with a classmate until you get off work. One of the others might be glad of a bit extra cash for keeping an eye on him.'

'The Lucases do not go cap in hand to other people, Viney, and that's all I have to say on the subject.'

'But what about me, Dad?' she

pleaded tearfully.

Neil took up his paper, and she could tell from the set of his jaw that it was no use trying to plead with him. His mind was made up.

Viney was in tears by the time she met up with George. 'It's no good, George! Dad won't hear of me leaving without Aidan. It's not fair! I've looked after him ever since Mum died, but I had no idea that Dad expected me to go on doing it for ever!'

'That's a bit much, isn't it? Never mind, I expect he'll come round when he's had more time to think.'

'He won't, George, I know him. Look, can't we take Aidan to Australia with us? He'd love it there, I'm sure.'

'You've got to be kidding! I've no intention of starting a marriage with a ready-made family!'

'But I thought you liked Aidan! You've always let him come with us on days out.'

'Sure, when it was a choice of seeing you or missing out because you had to babysit. But Australia? It's just not on. Australia may be the land of milk and honey but new arrivals like us can't expect to fall into cushy jobs and live like lords from the very beginning. If you and I go there together we'll both have to work at first, probably in rotten jobs to start with, until we get established. We'd be in a real bind with a kiddie in tow, and we couldn't expect Mum to take him on. She's finished bringing up kids and she's entitled to a bit of peace now.'

'Would you consider staying on in Llanidris for a while?' she said softly. 'We could go out to join your family later on, when Aidan is old enough to see to himself.'

'And how long will that be? Five years? Ten? It's too much to ask, Viney, and you know it.'

George was insistent that Aidan was Neil's responsibility and that it was ridiculous of Viney to even consider giving up her plans for him. As for Viney, in her mind's eye she could see her mother's white face on her death bed as she'd begged her to care for the boy. It had been easy for Viney to give her word in those circumstances. Now that it came to the crunch she couldn't break it, and that was the end of it.

When she heard Viney's story, Ceridwen was disgusted. 'Are you crazy?' she shrieked. 'Your Dad can't do this to you! If you had any sense you'd ignore him and marry George anyway. Elope or something.'

'You know I can't marry without Dad's consent until I'm twenty-one, and by that time it'll be too late. The Blaneys will have gone to Australia and I'll never see George again!'

'Have a bit of gumption, do! Get up to Gretna Green and do the deed. Don't be so feeble, Viney Lucas. I wouldn't be, if I were in your place!'

* * *

'I can't tell you how sorry I am,' Sybil wrote, when Viney poured out her heart

227

in a letter. 'Surely your George won't go off to Australia and leave you flat? Honestly, your dad doesn't have the right to do this to you. Do you want me to come down to Llanidris and tackle him about it?'

Viney managed a smile at the thought of Sybil arriving on the doorstep like an avenging angel.

In some ways she could understand her father. He had struggled on after losing his wife and depended on her to keep the home fires burning. He probably didn't know how to cope without her.

It was George who was the big disappointment, though. Firm in his resolve to travel out to Australia with his family, he promised they would keep in touch, and if she ever managed to get round Neil she could follow them out and they'd be married there, he said. She doubted this very much, however. After coming face to face with those bikini-clad beauties who were shown in all their glory in the pamphlets he would probably forget all about Viney and marry somebody else.

Right up to the last moment she hoped he would change his mind about going. He would sweep her into his arms, saying that he couldn't bear to leave her. However, when the day of departure came and went with no sign of him she was forced to accept that she had been abandoned, and her beautiful dream was ended.

Neil found her at the kitchen table, weeping inconsolably, and he put an arm round her shoulders in an awkward attempt at comfort.

'Weeping over your young man, love? Never mind, he's not worth it. If he really thought anything of you he'd have stayed put. This just shows him in his true colours. If you ask me, you've had a narrow escape.'

Viney fled to her room, not wanting to hear any more. Men! The worst of it was that there was something in what her dad said.

She lay on her bed for a long while

and then, having made up her mind to a course of action, she got up again, washed her face, and went out of the house. There was a queue of people waiting to use the telephone box outside the shop cum post office, but she waited doggedly until her turn came.

After using up all her change she finally got hold of Sybil and they managed to hatch a plan before the pips went.

'Hello, love. I didn't hear you go out,' Neil remarked when she got back to the house.

'I just went up to the call box at the shop. I've come to a decision, Dad. I'm going to London for a few days, starting tomorrow.'

His eyes narrowed. 'What are you up to, girl? You're not thinking of sneaking off to Australia, are you?'

There was a bitter note in Viney's voice as she reminded him that that had fallen through.

'It's because of that, though, that I

have to get away for a bit. Do you know that I've never had a holiday?'

'I suppose you haven't, love. Look, the next time I get a few days off I'll take you and Aidan to Barry Island for a treat. How will that be?'

'I'm sure Aidan will love it, Dad, but I still want to go to London.'

She was amazed to find herself telling him what she was about to do, rather than asking permission, but she realised that she had to assert herself if she wanted to get her own way.

The tactic seemed to work, for he went on to ask where she planned to stay, hotels in London being pricey if he knew anything about it.

'I've had a chat with Sybil, and I can stay with her.'

'At the hospital? Surely not.'

'No, at her flat. Third-year students are allowed to live out. The girl Sybil shared with has gone home for days off, so I can have her bed.'

'You seem to have it all arranged,' Neil admitted, 'but what about . . . '

Viney's eyes flashed. 'What about Aidan? That's what you were going to say, isn't it? Well, arrangements will have to be made for him while I'm gone, because I'm certainly not taking him with me!'

She half expected to be sent to her room without her supper for answering back like that, but it must have sunk in that she was grown up now and no longer subject to that sort of discipline. Or perhaps he understood that he had to loosen the reins a bit if he wanted to keep her at home as a housekeeper and childminder.

Still, it wasn't until her journey was well under way that she was able to relax and look forward to the holiday.

It was true that she had never had one; the war had seen to that. The older boys had stories of having been taken to the seaside before she was born. They'd been given brightly-coloured buckets and spades and had a marvellous time making sandcastles and having donkey rides on the beach. In her day all the beaches had been blocked off with barbed wire and other barricades, meant to deter the enemy, trying to invade from across the Channel. Everything was back to normal now, of course, but so much else had intervened in the meantime.

First there had been her father's need to adjust to civilian life. He had been morose for much of the time, often getting up in the night to go for long walks while all Llanidris was sound asleep. Laura's time had been taken up with organising the children so that they led as normal a life as possible while the house was kept quiet. He had been apt to jump at any loud noise and they had all learned to tiptoe about like mice, only behaving noisily when he was off at work.

Time had done its healing work, however, and they had became a normal family again, and then Aidan had came on the scene. A colicky baby who roared his displeasure at all hours of the day and night, he had been another reason for holidays being out of the question. No boarding-house landlady would have welcomed such a disruption!

'One day,' Laura would sigh, when her older children begged to go to Swansea or Barry Island, but that day had never come.

Now Viney was actually on her way to London she had a long list of places she wanted to see, gleaned from a glossy picture book she'd brought home from the library. Westminster Abbey, the Tower, St Paul's Cathedral, Madame Tussaud's, Trafalgar Square, the Regent's Park zoo! And could she squeeze in a visit to Kew Gardens?

'I thought you'd never get here!' Sybil gushed when the train arrived. 'Do you want to go back to the flat, or we could make a start on your sight-seeing tour right away, if you like.'

Sybil looked much more mature than when Viney had seen her last. Perhaps it was an air of confidence, the result of her nurse's training? But then, she'd always been brimming with confidence, even as a child. Perhaps the good fairies had given her that gift at her christening.

'I know what it is,' Viney said suddenly. 'You've put your hair up!'

'Oh, yes,' Sybil laughed, fingering her chignon. 'I have to wear it up when I'm on the wards, and now I rather like it. St Martha's is just like the army, you know; it's the worst kind of sin to go about with your hair touching your collar.'

'Tell me about this fiancé of yours.'

'Derek? Oh, you'll be meeting him soon enough and you can see for yourself. It's the annual hospital dance tomorrow and we'll all be going to that. I'll find you something to wear.'

'Oh, I don't know if I'm up to it. Anyway, you'll want to go with Derek. I can find something to do at the flat.'

'You certainly will not! I know what the matter is; you're remembering those ghastly hops at Llanidris, with everyone jiving all over the place. This is St

Martha's; it's much more sedate. Everyone goes, from the governors and the consultants down to the newest student.'

* * *

Viney wasn't sure what to make of Derek. He was tall and thin, with a face like a rather unhappy horse, although, as she hastily reminded herself, looks weren't everything, and it wasn't important if she didn't find him attractive. He was Sybil's choice, not hers.

Nor did he have much to say for himself, although he listened gloomily to all that was said and Sybil had told her that he was a gifted individual, possibly bordering on genius. His lips did curve into a smile whenever he looked at Sybil, though, so probably he was different when he was alone with her. Viney summed him up as being shy.

The dance was to be held in the

hospital boardroom, a cavernous place that had been a ward when St Martha's was first built, in the mid-nineteenth century. Now it had a low dais at one end, where on the night a band would be playing, and trestle tables were being set up along one wall when Sybil and Viney peeped inside. Several off-duty nurses were busily putting up paper chains and balloons and a porter arrived with a clanking trolley full of glasses and plates.

Privately Viney thought it would take more than a few balloons and a fruit drink to make the room appear more than the draughty old barracks it really was, so when they turned up on the night she was pleasantly surprised by the transformation. Lively music provided a background to the buzz of conversation, and a great many people stood around with drinks in their hands, waiting for the dancing to start.

Viney had borrowed a circular skirt in cerise-coloured felt, worn over a crinoline petticoat, and although the white satin blouse wasn't what she would have bought for herself, she had to admit that she didn't look half bad. Sybil had done her dark hair up in curlers for her and applied some discreet makeup which had gone a long way towards boosting Viney's self confidence.

'No, you won't be a wallflower here,' Sybil had assured her. 'You wouldn't anyway, looking like that, but in any case, the senior doctors make it a point to dance with everyone so nobody is left out. That's the beauty of working in a place like this; we're like a family.'

A portly middle-aged man had now taken his place on the dais and was singing songs from throughout the decade in a beautiful tenor voice. She had just fallen under the spell of *Once I Had A Secret Love* when she felt a tap on the shoulder and turned to see a good-looking man looking at her somewhat hesitantly.

'I say, haven't we met somewhere before?'

Viney was about to summon up a witty retort to this old chestnut when recognition dawned. 'Aren't you the doctor who came to Llanidris as Dr Foy's locum?'

'Yes, and now I remember where I've seen you before. You brought a little boy to see me. Andrew, was it?'

'Aidan. My little brother. You discovered he needed specs.'

'How is he doing now?'

'His school work has come on by leaps and bounds since he got them. He's still a bit of a live-wire, though. Apparently he'll be going into a class with a male teacher next year, and we're hoping he may respond better to that. His current one is a lovely grandmotherly type who never raises her voice and my father feels she isn't strict enough with him. But what about you? Do you work at St Martha's, Dr Russell?'

'Call me Tom.'

'And I'm Viney. Viney Lucas.'

'Hello again, Viney. Yes, I'm a

Martha's man. I'm thinking of moving into general practice one of these days, though. Possibly some country place where I can bring up my children without worrying what they're up to when I take my eye off them for five minutes.'

Viney felt a pang of disappointment. 'How many children do you have?'

He laughed. 'None, yet! I'm not even married. I'm just looking ahead to the future. And what about you? I gather you're not married yet either, or your husband would never let you loose at a dance filled with lustful med students.'

'I'm engaged, actually. At least, I think I am.'

Tom laughed again. 'Don't you know? Either you are or you aren't.' He glanced at her left hand. 'I see you're not wearing a ring.'

'I was supposed to get one on my twenty-first birthday,' she told him. 'Meanwhile, my fiancé decided to move to Australia with his family, so things are a bit up in the air at the moment.

George wanted us to get married before they left so I could go with him, but there was Aidan to think of, so we had to put it off.'

Tom was easy to talk to, but loyalty to George kept her from saying anything more.

At that moment a dancing couple bumped into them, saying sorry before moving off.

'I think we're in the way here, Viney. Care to take a turn on the dance floor?'

He was a good dancer and she was able to relax in his arms as he expertly manoeuvred her around the ballroom. The floor had been treated with French chalk to make it slippery, and she glided about it as if she had been dancing all her life.

This happy state of affairs ended when another young man tapped Tom on the shoulder and Viney found herself partnered by someone who was in need of a few lessons. After he had stepped on her feet a number of times she was about to make an excuse to leave him when the music came to an end and she was saved.

'You're a fast worker!' Sybil said, when she and Derek joined her at the refreshment table. 'Two dances in a row, and how on earth did you manage to get hold of the dishy Dr Russell?'

'We've met before. He remembered me,' Viney said smugly, amused when Sybil's eyebrows shot up in surprise. 'Do you remember me telling you about taking Aidan to the doctor that time, only it turned out to be a locum, not our usual GP?'

'Vaguely, but I don't think you told me the man's name. Or if you did, I'd have had no reason to connect him with Tom Russell here.'

'I'd better go and have a dance with Natalie,' Derek interrupted. 'You don't mind, do you, Syb? She's sitting all alone over there.'

'Of course not. Go ahead and enjoy yourself.'

Sybil's eyes were sparkling and Viney thought she looked beautiful. She was wearing a pretty cotton frock with a three-tiered skirt and although she had explained that it had been purchased at Marks & Spencer she wore it with such aplomb that it might have come from a top fashion house. Her diamond engagement ring sparkled in the flashing lights and she wore matching earrings.

'These were a gift from Derek, too,' she'd explained earlier, when they were dressing. 'Paste, of course, but good, don't you think?'

Viney agreed that they would fool any untrained eye.

'Who's Natalie?' she asked now. 'And why does Derek think he has to dance with her?'

'Oh, they work together in the lab,' Sybil explained. 'She's supposed to be quite brilliant but outside of work she's a bit of a mouse. She never has much to say for herself. She can't help being plain, but she makes no effort to make the best of herself. I think Derek feels sorry for her, really.' She nudged Viney with her elbow. 'Tom Russell's coming this way. I bet he's going to ask you for another dance!'

Viney blushed, but she managed to summon up a smile before taking to the floor with the young doctor. The singer was now crooning softly, and she relaxed in Tom's arms, with her head on his shoulder. 'If I give my heart to you, will you handle it with care . . . '

She wasn't about to give her heart to anyone but George, of course, but the sweet words of the song worked their magic, and she was content to live in the moment, pretending that all was right with her world. In two days' time she could be back in Llanidris, living her dull life with nothing exciting to look forward to. Meanwhile, she would enjoy herself thoroughly, building up happy memories to sustain her through the years ahead.

If only she had been dancing with George at this moment her cup of happiness would have been full, but by now he was thousands of miles away and she might never see him again. She pushed the thought away from her and concentrated on what Tom was murmuring in her ear.

# Shocks For All

'What did you get up to while I was away?' Viney said, holding the little parcel behind her back while Aidan tried to snatch it from her.

'What did you bring me? I want to see!'

'Don't be rude, Aidan. Answer me first. Did you do anything special while I was away in London?'

'Dad and Matt and me went out for tea.'

'Did you really? Where did you go?'

'Went to Effoo's. We had beans on toast.'

Viney handed him the package which he tore open to reveal a Dinky toy, one of a series which he loved to collect. He sat down on the floor at once and began to push it along, making 'vroom vroom' noises.

'Who on earth is Effoo?' Viney asked

Matt, who had come into the room to see what all the noise was about. He laughed.

'He means Ethel. Ceridwen's mother. She runs the tea-room.'

'Aidan says you went there to have beans on toast. I've never known Dad to eat away from home, but why now? You can have beans at home.'

Matt turned red. 'I was supposed to cook, but the toast went on fire when I wasn't looking and there wasn't any more bread in the house.'

'So Dad decided you'd better find someone who knew how to cook?'

If possible, Matt's face crimsoned even further. 'It was Ceridwen's idea actually. I was trying to impress her but I should have stuck with ham sandwiches and shop-bought cake!'

'What was she doing here? Won't Brenda mind?'

'Oh, that's all off. She's a nice girl but we just didn't click. The feeling was mutual. Anyway, Ceridwen's mum put on a very nice meal, even if Aidan did insist on having beans instead of what we were having. He said he'd been looking forward to them.'

Viney didn't ask how Matt had come together with Ceridwen. She was fond of her eldest brother and she only hoped that the girl wasn't using him to make Dai Williams jealous. She sighed. Why was life so full of thorns?

'Was there any post for me, Matt?'

He shook his head. 'Are you expecting to hear from George? He'd better not send you a postcard saying 'Wish you were here'. Is it all over between you two, Viney?'

'I wish I knew. We parted on frosty terms, as you might imagine, but we didn't break off our engagement as such. If I'd had a ring to fling back in his face it might have been different. Now I'm wondering if I'd have shouted and wailed whether he might have backed down and stayed with me.'

'And then resented you for ever after. No, if he'd made up his mind to go it was just as well you were able to maintain your dignity.' He gazed into the distance for a moment before speaking again. 'How's Sybil? Getting along all right, is she?'

'Happy as a lark. She's almost finished her training, and she's looking forward to getting married and settling down.'

'I'm glad she's happy,' he said softly, but his eyes were sad and Viney's heart ached for him.

Her holiday in London had done her good. Miles away from home, she'd been able to see things in a different light and she knew she had to take charge of her life, even if marriage wasn't on the cards. She would insist that she had to get out more in the evenings, even if her father had to cough up for a sitter for Aidan. He surely owed her that much.

The town was only a short bus ride away; she could take up roller skating, perhaps, or go to evening classes. If she could learn to sew properly she could get out her mum's old Singer and update her wardrobe; it shouldn't be too hard to produce a pretty dress or two.

'You could join our rambling club,' John said eagerly, when he heard her mentioning this to Neil. 'It doesn't cost much, and all you need is a good pair of boots or walking shoes. We go to some interesting places, and sometimes we team up with the Birdwatchers' Association and they point out interesting birds as we go along.'

'That sounds like a good idea,' Neil put in. 'You don't get enough fresh air, my girl, cooped up in the house all day. You go along with John this Saturday and see how you like it.'

So Viney went, hoping that the ever-present Aidan wouldn't lag behind grumbling, but he strode out at the front of the group, pleased to be doing something with John and his mates.

The experiment was a success, and Viney paid the modest subscription and became a fully-fledged member.

All that walking lifted her spirits and, as a bonus, improved her figure.

★　★　★

When, at long last, a letter came from George, she was in better frame of mind to read it without breaking down. It contained no hint of an apology but at least he spoke as if they still meant something to each other, which was some comfort.

'But he could at least have said he was sorry for leaving me,' she grumbled to Matt. More and more these days she was confiding in him. 'He seems to think that I was in the wrong in all this.'

'I can't say I blame him, Vine. It was asking too much of him to expect him to take on Aidan as part of the package.'

'You would have, if you were in his place.'

'That's where you're wrong. I wouldn't want to take on another man's child.'

Viney stared at him as if seeing him for the first time. 'Matt Lucas! You mean if you met a young widow you wouldn't want her children? That's horrible!'

'That's different. Aidan isn't your child, he's your brother. Dad should never have expected you to sacrifice your life for him. I told him that at the time. We had words over it, in fact.'

Viney's jaw dropped. 'I didn't know that.'

'Well, you wouldn't. We were out in the woods at the time. I did my best for you, but I might as well have tried to shift the Rock of Gibraltar. Of course, there was a bit more to it than that. He thought you were too young to get married. It might have been different if George had moved into the house here as Dad suggested, but going off to Australia with these Blaneys — whom he hasn't even met, incidentally — seemed like flying too far from the nest.'

These revelations put a different slant

on the situation, but it didn't do much to heal the hurt that still filled her heart and mind. How dare Dad treat her like this! On the one hand she was expected to behave like the grown woman she very nearly was, running a busy household and caring for a little boy, and on the other she was too young to cope with life in a new country, even with a husband to support her.

For a while she let her correspondence with Sybil lapse. She didn't want to fill her letters with endless moaning; her friend knew the situation and had already offered all the consolation she could give. Then, too, the important final exams were looming, and Sybil was determined to do well. If she passed all her courses, and completed her three years of service to St Martha's, she would become a State Registered Nurse, entitled to wear the little enamelled badge which proclaimed her proud status.

'I'll be in touch again once the dust settles,' she wrote. 'If only they'd give us time off to study I'd be OK, but it's hard to buckle down after tramping up and down the wards all day. At least the girls on nights can do their swotting in the small hours if nothing's going on.'

So the months passed, with Viney beginning to feel more cheerful. And then the blow fell.

'Effoo!' Aidan wriggled down from the table where he was wrestling with his homework, and Viney looked up to see her father and Ceridwen's mother standing in the doorway, beaming.

Neil cleared his throat. 'Are Matt and John anywhere about? Ethel and I — er — we have something to tell you all.'

'Out in the garden, I think, Dad. I'll go and call them,' Viney said.

Once they were all there, their father draped his arm across Ethel's shoulders, a silly grin on his face.

'Ethel has done me the honour of agreeing to marry me, and I hope you'll all be very pleased,' Neil announced, beaming.

After a moment's stunned hesitation

Matt stepped forward and shook his father by the hand. 'Congratulations, Dad! I hope you'll be very happy together.'

'Me, too,' John said. 'Hope you'll be happy, I mean.'

Neil turned to his daughter. 'How about you, then, Viney?'

'Of course,' she muttered. 'I didn't know that you were, em, seeing Mrs Hughes.'

'You must call me Ethel,' the woman said with a smile. 'I don't suppose you'll want to call me Mam, but I'll do my best to keep everyone happy.'

Viney flinched. How could anybody be happy after a shock like this? Their dad must have been seeing Ethel in the evenings after work, when he was supposed to be at the Red Dragon.

'I think this calls for a glass of something,' Neil smiled, rubbing his hands together. 'Will you do the honours, Matt?'

Here was another innovation. Although Neil enjoyed the odd pint at the pub, drinking in the home was reserved for Christmas Day, when the family toasted the Queen. Now apparently even Aidan was to be allowed a thimbleful of sherry which he immediately spat out, pulling a face.

As soon as she could escape Viney rushed upstairs and threw herself down on her bed, needing a good cry. Unfortunately, however, some things strike too deeply for tears and that relief didn't come to her. After a while she got up and tiptoed down the stairs, slipping out of the back door unnoticed.

All was quiet in the churchyard except for the cooing of a solitary dove. She made her way to her mother's grave and knelt down, rocking back and forth until the tears came at last.

'Oh, Mum!' she sobbed. 'I can't believe it. Dad came home tonight and announced he's getting married. I don't think you knew her; her name's Ethel Hughes and she runs a tea-shop down by the bus stop. I went to school with her daughter, Ceridwen. In fact, I still go around with her quite a lot.'

A thought struck Viney. When Neil and Ethel married, Ceridwen would become her step-sister. What would happen then? Would she come to join them in Lilac Lane? That would mean sharing a bedroom. Viney couldn't bear it. She liked Ceridwen, of course, but the prospect of too much change all at once was daunting.

She liked to think that her mother was looking down from Heaven, watching over her family. Laura would probably be pleased for Neil, who had been lonely since her death. Viney wished that she could be similarly understanding, but it was hard.

Her way back home took her past the main door of the church and on impulse she stepped inside. The old building was cool and welcoming, and she sank down in a pew, hoping that peace would come . . .

She came to with a start to find the vicar standing at her side.

'Is everything all right, Viney?'

'I had a bit of a shock this evening, Mr Smart.'

'Oh yes? May I venture a guess, my dear? This has something to do with your father's remarriage, hasn't it?'

'How did you know?'

'They called here earlier to see when I might be able to perform the wedding. Your father hasn't been very regular in his attendance since coming back from the war but he does want to get married here, in the church he attended as a boy.'

Viney felt a lump in her throat. If things had been different she would have stood in front of the altar here when she married George.

The vicar was mouthing platitudes now. Neil was still a comparatively young man with many years ahead of him. He had been a good husband, 'till death do us part', but he had been widowed for several years now and it was time to move on. His children would leave home in due course

— Mark had already gone — and he would be alone. It was good that he had found someone with whom to spend his twilight years.

Viney nodded and gave the answers he obviously wanted to hear, but inside she was seething with indignation. What about her? Nobody had stopped to think of what this would mean to her!

On the road home she met Matt, who greeted her with some relief. 'There you are! I've been looking for you.'

'I went up to Mum's grave.'

'I thought so. This thing with Dad has upset you, hasn't it?' He shrugged. 'If it's what he wants, more power to him, I say. Anyway, I won't be stopping at home much longer. It's about time I left the nest.'

'That's what the vicar said. About everyone growing up and leaving, I mean. But what about me, Matt? Where am I going to go?'

'I don't think Dad expects you to go anywhere. This is your home for as long as you want it. The difference is, you won't have to work so hard with Ethel there to share the load.'

'And wanting to do things her way as mistress of the house.'

Matt shook his head, looking perplexed. There were some things that men just couldn't seem to understand.

There was only one thing left to do. That night she poured out her feelings in a long letter to Sybil.

'I know I'm being beastly, and I really do mean to do my best to welcome Ethel into the family. That's her name, Ethel Hughes; she's the mother of my friend Ceridwen. She's quite nice really, although, of course, she's not Mum. I should be pleased for Dad, but why couldn't this have happened sooner?

'He stopped me marrying George because I was needed at home, and now suddenly I'm a spare wheel! I made that sacrifice for nothing, Sybil, and nobody seems to appreciate it. Even Aidan wouldn't miss me if I suddenly disappeared. He's really taken to Ethel and she seems fond of him. Oh, why does life have to be so complicated?'

Sybil's training had come to an end, and she wrote to tell Viney all about the ceremony in which she had received her diploma and the gold medal for surgical nursing from the hands of the Duchess of Kent.

'Hearing me talk about weddings is probably the last thing you need now,' she wrote, 'but mine is in the works at last and I want you to come to London to help me finalise the details. Mum's a great help, of course, but she doesn't know a thing about music and the organist is getting impatient to know what we've chosen.

'We also have to measure you for your dress and there isn't much time. Are you really sure you want blue? Dusty rose would suit you so much better with your colouring, but it's up to you. I did promise you that you could decide for yourself, being the only bridesmaid. I do insist on choosing the style, though. I don't want you outshining the bride!'

Not much chance of that, Viney thought.

Another letter followed soon afterwards. 'I'm glad you've seen sense and plan to spend a nice long time here. I'm at home with Mum, of course, so you won't have to pig it in the nurses' quarters. Let me know when you're arriving and I'll be there to meet you. Oh, and guess what!' Viney turned to the next page, intrigued. 'Derek didn't know who to ask to be Best Man. He doesn't have a brother or a cousin, and he doesn't know any of the lab technicians well enough. So he told me I'd have to find one for him. Did you ever hear such nonsense? So anyway, I went and found Tom Russell, and he said he'd be honoured to do it! He was a bit hesitant at first, until I told him who the only bridesmaid is going to be, and then he jumped at it. Am I a clever girl, or what?'

Smiling, Viney found herself agreeing.

★ ★ ★

All the rushing around was over at last. The church had been decorated, the wedding gifts had been put on display in the Waites' home, and a marquee had been erected in the back garden. The caterers had come with boxes of glasses and plates. Sybil's father, home on leave for the occasion, had double checked on the band who were to play following the wedding breakfast.

'Although why they call it that is beyond me,' Daisy Waite laughed, 'especially when the wedding is in the afternoon with a sit-down meal to follow.'

Sybil was blissfully happy. 'I wouldn't care if it was a picnic!'

'I don't suppose you would, darling. I'm only sorry that Laura couldn't have been spared to see this day. After everything she did during the war she was a second mother to you. I can never thank her enough.'

Assorted relatives from both sides had converged on London and were staying in hotels. Friends of the bride and groom hadn't so far to come because they were mostly St Martha's people. Sybil had invited the Lucas men, whom she looked on as her foster brothers, but all had declined, Mark because he simply wasn't interested, John because he was too shy and Matt — well, Viney could guess why that was.

She had purchased a set of matching sheets and pillowcases which, according to her carefully-written label, had come from all the boys, but that was the closest any of them came to actually attending the event. A pity, really, but Sybil would have eyes for her bride-groom alone. Nobody else mattered.

Daisy Waite had organised a small party for the out-of-town family members, and this took place at the house so that her daughter could retire early.

'You want to look your best tomorrow,' she warned.

'Oh, Mum! I'm not getting married until two o'clock. I can have a lovely long lie-in.'

'That's what you think! The hairdresser's coming at ten, and I don't care what you say, you're going to have a good breakfast. I don't want you fainting coming down the aisle!'

The Waites' relatives, although all very pleasant, were strangers to Viney, so when Sybil retired for the night, she elected to turn in as well.

She tossed and turned for a long time before finally falling asleep and then her rest was disturbed by garbled dreams. Perhaps it was the effect of being in a strange bed, or maybe she had eaten too much at the party.

She awoke in the morning feeling fuzzy headed; with any luck a cool shower would put her to rights.

People were coming and going in all directions when the doorbell rang.

'That'll be the hairdresser,' Daisy

panted. 'I thought she'd never get here! She's got all three of us to see to. I hope she's left enough time.'

She bustled off to answer the door. A moment later they heard her raised voice saying, 'You can't see her now, it's bad luck!'

'Who is it, Mum?'

Daisy put her head round the door. 'It's Derek,' she hissed. 'I've told him to go away but he insists on speaking to you!'

'It's all right, Mum, tell him to come in. I think the bad luck bit only applies when I'm in my wedding dress, but I'm still in my dressing-gown!'

Looking very stern, Daisy ushered the bridegroom in. He hovered in the doorway, looking pointedly at Viney.

'I need to speak to you, Sybil. Alone.

'Oh, can't this wait?' Daisy was becoming crosser by the minute. 'The hairdresser will be here at any minute. We don't have time for this.'

'I'm sorry, Mrs Waite. This is important. Would you mind leaving us alone for just a little while?'

'Oh, very well. Just get it over with as quickly as possible, will you?'

'No, Viney, I want you to stay,' Sybil ordered, as Viney made to follow Daisy out to the hall. 'I have a feeling I'm going to need some support.' She sank down into a squashy armchair and faced Derek calmly. 'Well, go on then. What can be so important that you need to burst in on us when we're sitting here half dressed?'

Taking a deep breath, Derek said his piece. 'I'm so sorry, Sybil, I can't tell you just how sorry I am, but I've realised I can't go through with this. I can't marry you.'

'There's somebody else, I suppose.' Sybil's voice was low and icy.

'Yes, I'm afraid there is, but not in the way you mean.'

'Natalie?'

He swallowed hard. 'You mustn't think we've been having an affair or anything like that. We haven't even been out for a meal together, unless you count sitting at the same table in the hospital canteen.'

'But you've worked together for years, sometimes late into the night.' Sybil nodded. 'And you've suddenly come to the realisation that once we're married Natalie will be lost to you for good, and so you've come to your senses before it's too late. Is that it?'

'Basically, yes,' Derek agreed.

Viney raised her eyebrows. Poor Sybil sounded like the heroine of a Victorian novel, but it seemed that she'd hit the nail on the head, for Derek was nodding like an idiot.

Sybil grunted in disgust. She wrenched off her engagement ring and slapped it into his palm.

'You've said what you came to say, so you'd better be off. As Mum said, we're expecting the hairdresser at any minute and we mustn't keep her waiting.'

'She must be hysterical,' Viney told herself as Derek made his escape. 'None of us is going to need a hair-do now,' but Sybil seemed quite self-contained.

'What on earth was all that about?' Daisy demanded, fluttering back into the room. 'And where is that wretched woman? I'll have something to say if she makes us all late!'

'It doesn't matter, Mum. Nothing matters, really. The wedding's off. I'm not getting married after all. That's what Derek came to tell me.'

'What are you talking about? Of course there's going to be a wedding! Everything's arranged! All the guests are here! Old Great-Aunt Bessie's come all the way from Yorkshire!'

'It's true, Mrs Waite,' Viney put in. 'Derek came to break it off. That's why he had to come now; it couldn't wait until later.'

'This is ridiculous nonsense! John! John! Go after him and see what this is all about!'

Sybil waved her father way, saying they'd tell him all about it later.

'No, come here, John. You'll have to

give me a hand.' Daisy had pulled herself together and was thinking of the thousand and one things that had to be done if the wedding was cancelled. There was the vicar to be notified, the guests to be sent away, the caterers to be stopped . . .

'Hang on, old girl.' As a naval officer, John Waite had long ago learned to think on his feet in times of crisis. 'We've got all these people looking forward to a good meal, and we'll be stuck with the catering bill in any case, so why not let that aspect of things go forward?

'I'll ring the vicar and ask him to make an announcement when everyone's there, telling people to come here as planned. Of course, they'll all turn up early, looking for a stiff drink. There's nothing but wine here and the champagne was meant for the toasts, so I'd better pop down to the off licence and lay in supplies of the hard stuff. In fact, I could do with a snifter right now!'

'Pour one for me!' Daisy said.

Left alone with Sybil, Viney struggled to find something useful to say, and came up with nothing.

'I suppose all those toast racks and butter dishes will have to be packed up and sent back,' Sybil said at last. 'Not that I care, really. Who needs five butter dishes?'

'Tell everyone to take their gifts away with them after the meal,' Viney said idiotically. 'That'll save on postage.'

She mentally kicked herself. Here they were, discussing the best way of returning presents, when what really mattered was that Sybil's world was in ruins. But what else could they do? She really wanted to kick and scream, for her own sake as well as Sybil's, but what good would that do?

'We're a bright pair, aren't we?' Sybil said, dabbing at her blotched face with a tear-soaked tissue. 'There must be something wrong with us, both left in the lurch like this. I suppose life will go on eventually, although I can't see how at the moment. The question is, what are we going to do now?'

*   *   *

'I could kill that Derek!' Daisy said, for the umpteenth time. 'Letting you down at the last minute like that, after all the trouble and expense everyone had gone to to make sure you had a perfect day.'

It was the day after the drama and all the guests had left for home.

'Oh, it might have been worse,' Sybil sighed.

'Worse? I don't see how!'

'He didn't leave me standing at the altar, as they say. At least he had the gumption to come and let me know before I went through all that rigmarole of turning up at the church on Dad's arm.'

'I should think so, too!' Daisy looked so fierce that both girls burst out laughing.

'I don't know what's so funny, I'm sure,' she protested.

'You, Mum. You look like that cat of Mrs Bruce's next door, when she dares to present it with tinned food instead of poached salmon.'

'Well, really!' But Daisy saw the funny side of it and barked with laughter and before they knew it they were all rolling helplessly in their chairs.

When they had sobered up, Sybil remarked that if things had been otherwise, she'd have been sunning herself on a Caribbean beach by now, and that set Daisy off again.

'It's Derek that'll be out of pocket over that, thank goodness. Not like us with all the expenses that come with being the bride's family.'

'Unless he's taken Natalie on our honeymoon instead! Derek's the thrifty type. He wouldn't let all that money go to waste.'

'He wouldn't dare!' Daisy snapped, but as none of them knew just what Derek would dare her remark went unanswered.

'I do think it would be a good idea

for you to get away for a break, though, darling. What with one thing and another we're not too flush at the moment, but I'm sure we could manage something closer to home. What about the Lake District, for instance? Is there any chance you could go with her, Viney?'

'Actually, Mum, I think I'd like to go to Llanidris, if Viney will have me. Some of the happiest days of my life were spent in Wales, despite the war. It's so peaceful there, and peace is what I need right now.'

'Of course you can come,' Viney said at once. 'Dad'll love to see you.'

'Will there be room?'

'Just as long as you're willing to move in with me. Ethel won't be moving in until after they're married, of course, so it'll be like old times, except that Mark won't be around.'

Sybil laughed. 'I was besotted with Mark when I was a teenager, and I was so upset when he dropped me. I wonder how many poor girls he's had on his string since then?'

'Dozens I expect. When you do want to leave?'

'Let's go tonight. Do you mind, Mum? The only thing is, how can we let Uncle Neil know in time when you're not on the phone at home?'

'Don't worry about Dad. I told him to expect me when he saw me, and we can always fit one more person round the kitchen table. He might not even be home when we arrive. When he's not working on the estate he spends every waking moment with his Effoo, as Aidan calls her.'

# Happy Ever Afters

'Syboo!' Aidan flung his arms round the visitor, stepping on her toes in the process.

'Steady on, young man, you'll have me over. I'm surprised you remember me after all this time.'

He giggled. 'Did you bring me a present?'

'Yes, I did. A big chunk of wedding cake, all covered in royal icing.'

John's eyes lit up. 'Did you really? Can I have a bit now? Aidan's eaten all the biscuits and I'm starving.'

In the circumstances Daisy had refused to serve the cake at the reception, but had kept it for their own use. She had given the bottom layer to Sybil to take with her to Llanidris.

'Where's my present?' Aidan persisted.

Viney tried to look stern. 'You

mustn't ask, Aidan, or you won't get!
I've told you that before.' Then she
spoiled the lesson by reaching into her
handbag and bringing out a toy police
car. To this Sybil added a miniature
ambulance, explaining how people
arrived at St Martha's casualty department to be made better after they'd had
an accident.

'I'd like to go for a walk this evening
and see what's changed,' Sybil announced.

'Llanidris is just the same as when
you left it,' Viney told her. 'They should
change its name to Brigadoon! Where
would you like to go?'

'Up to the fairy well, if that's all
right.'

So they walked up to the fairy well,
which was a tiny spring flowing from
the hillside above the village. Historians
believed that it had been there for
hundreds of years; the locals no longer
believed in fairies, of course, but they
did go and drop a pin into its depths
when there was something they particularly wanted.

'Are you going to wish for Derek to change his mind?' Viney asked softly.

'Oh, no, I shan't do that,' Sybil replied. 'I didn't know it was possible to hurt so much, and it may be that I'll never get over him, but if he hadn't had the courage to call it off we might have lived in misery for years, or at least that's what Mum tells me. There's never been a divorce in our family, and I've no wish to start a trend.'

'Do you hate Natalie very much?'

Sybil thought for a long moment. 'Not really. We can't help who we fall in love with, can we? Come to that, I've no idea if she even likes Derek. It may be all on his side.'

'Do you hope they'll come together now he's free?'

'I think it's too early to say that, Viney. What about you and George? Do you still love him?'

'At first I thought I'd die when he went away,' she confessed, 'but now I find myself going for hours at a time without even thinking of him. I wonder if it was just first love after all. They say you never forget it, although it isn't the real thing in the end.'

'That's too bad, because I was thinking we might go out to Australia together. Before I met Derek I used to dream of seeing the world after I qualified. I've given in my notice at St Martha's; as you know they don't allow married nurses in hospital. Nobody could work the hours we do and do justice to a home and family as well. Now I'm footloose and fancy-free I can travel anywhere I choose, and Australia is as good a place to start as any. Your family doesn't need you now, so you can come too. I thought that you and George could marry over there if that's what you still wanted to do, but now it sounds as if you've changed your mind.'

'I don't know what I want, Sybil. I'd hate to get all the way over there only to find I don't feel the same about him any more. To tell you the truth, I feel really let down by what he did. It wasn't just Dad, you know. He had his reasons for what he made me do, but George? He could have stayed behind with me and joined the Blaneys later but he didn't. How reliable does that make him?'

Sybil threw her pin into the water but she refused to say what her wish had been. They walked back to Lilac Lane, talking about other things. There were so many memories of their shared girlhood in Llanidris that they were never likely to run out of things to talk about.

Matt was at home when they finally returned. His face lit up when he saw Sybil. Viney peered around for Ceridwen so she could introduce her two friends to each other, but she wasn't there.

'Ceridwen? Oh, we're not seeing each other any more. She's tied up with Dai Williams now. She's been chasing after him for a long time.'

'I'm sorry,' Sybil told him.

He grinned. 'I'm not!'

'Does this mean she won't be coming

here to live when Dad and Ethel get married?' Viney said hopefully. 'I've heard that Dai's the jealous type. I don't know what he'd think about Ceridwen living under the same roof as an old flame, and as she's so keen on him she won't want to rock the boat.'

'I had an idea about that,' he smiled, 'but I've changed my mind. I've just had a flash of inspiration, and I think you'll like what I have to say! How about the cottage hospital?' Matt turned to Sybil. 'John filled me in on what happened, with your marriage falling through. I thought you might not want to stay on at St Martha's, where everyone knows about it. Too much sympathy can be hard to take. So why not stay around here? There's a piece in this week's paper about the hospital trying to recruit nurses and I'm sure they'd be glad to take you on there.'

'Matt, what a wonderful idea! How about it, Sybil?'

'As a matter of fact I've already

handed in my notice in London, Matt, and Viney and I were just discussing what my next move will be. I'll certainly give it some thought.'

'There's something else. The advertisement says that staff can live in or live out, so why don't you and Viney get somewhere together?' He pulled a funny face at his sister. 'You'll be surplus to requirements when our stepmamma comes, and you may want to think of taking a job. There's not much on offer in these parts, but you'd have more opportunities in the town. How does that grab you?'

'It's wonderful! Do you think Dad will let me?'

'Phooey! You're almost twenty-one, Sis. What's he going to do, keep you locked up in the cupboard under the stairs? Anyway, he'll be too busy with Ethel to even notice you've gone!'

Sybil and Viney looked at each other. Why hadn't they thought of this? It could solve all their problems. They could build a new life together and still return to Lilac Lane whenever they felt like it.

'You can come with me to the hospital tomorrow, Viney, and I'll put in an application,' Sybil promised. 'I've got a good feeling about this.'

'So have I,' Matt said under his breath, but neither girl heard him.

* * *

As he had predicted, Neil put no obstacles in Viney's way and she accompanied Sybil to the cottage hospital in the town.

Much to their surprise, Matron was willing to see Sybil at once and Viney waited for her in the corridor outside her office. Matron was clearly impressed with Sybil's credentials but seemed puzzled as to why she was applying to this small rural hospital.

'It would amount to quite a step down for you, Nurse Waite, after your varied experience at St Martha's. May I enquire why you are interested in coming here after training in London?'

Sybil had no intention of giving Matron a tale of woe, so she simply said that she felt like a change of pace after the hurly burly of London.

'I spent the war years in Llanidris as an evacuee, and I've kept in touch with my foster family. I mean to share living accommodation with my friend who is still in the area.'

'How lovely.' Matron smiled. 'One hears so many horror stories about those days that it's nice to know that your experience was so satisfactory. Is your friend a nurse as well?'

'Sadly, no. As it happens we'd meant to enter St Martha's together, but then her mother died and she was needed at home to care for the younger children. She had to leave school at the age of sixteen although fortunately she was able to sit her O-levels and did quite well. Her father is about to remarry, which leaves her free to take a job for the first time.'

'I wonder if she's interested in office

work, Nurse Waite?'

'I should think she might be; why do you ask?'

'We've had a series of junior clerks in the front office, none of them satisfactory, I'm afraid. We just get them to the point where they're of some use to us when they move on to other things. A lack of maturity, I'm afraid. But your friend could be exactly what we're looking for.'

When Sybil came out into the hall she was bursting with excitement.

'You've landed the job?' Viney cried. 'Well done, you! Now, if only I can be as lucky, we'll be able to go searching for suitable flats.'

'You are!' Sybil was grinning like a Cheshire cat. 'There's a job for you here, if you want it. Not on the nursing side — in the office.'

Viney's face fell. 'But I didn't do Commercial. I can't type.'

'You won't have to. This is filing patient records and such. Matron says you should look in at the office on the way out and fill out an application. It's probably just a formality because none of the current school-leavers seems to fancy it.'

So they went back home feeling very pleased with themselves.

'I knew you'd get it,' Matt complimented Sybil.

'It's not just me,' she said proudly. 'It looks like Viney might have a job as well, in the hospital office. Isn't it wonderful?'

'Are you leaving, then?' Aidan wanted to know. 'Only, if you are, can I have your room? I'm sick of sharing with John, he's too bossy.'

'It'll all depend on whether Ceridwen comes to live here,' Viney said tartly. She was pretty sure that the girl would not, but after all she had done for Aidan she was miffed to find him speeding her on her way. Ungrateful little wretch!

'Now that you're staying in the area, perhaps we can go to the pictures occasionally,' Matt told Sybil, adding hastily, when he saw her face, 'as a threesome, I mean.'

He had waited a long time for his chance with her and he didn't want to spoil it now. After being let down just hours before her wedding, she wasn't about to rush into another relationship, that he knew. But if they saw enough of each other and he was careful not to put any pressure on her, who knew what might happen in time?

★ ★ ★

At Christmas they all sat in the front pews of All Saints' church to see their father married. He was dressed in a new blue suit, while Ethel wore a smart wool suit in deep cream and a hat that was so weighed down by artificial flowers and feathers that she had to keep pushing it higher up her brow.

Matt had been asked to serve as Best Man, and Ceridwen had condescended to attend her mother, though she confided to Viney that she felt a right fool standing there while her mother got married; the shoe should have been on the other foot.

'How's Dai?' Viney asked, not liking that way of talking about a perfectly nice mother, and she was grimly satisfied when Ceridwen pouted and said that she'd caught him two-timing her.

Ceridwen was fortunate to have a mother. Viney would have given anything to have Laura still with her, and that wasn't just because she'd had to sacrifice her own life in order to take her place in the home.

She was touched when the newlyweds stopped at Laura's grave and laid their boutonnières beside the headstone. Neil had been wearing a red rose and it comforted his daughter to see this little gesture, which to her meant that he had never forgotten his first wife, who would live on for ever in his heart. It was good that Ethel was in agreement with him on this, and romantic Viney believed that in placing her own pink carnation there she was silently telling Laura that she would take good care of her family.

She was delighted that Matt and Sybil were getting along so well with each other, and had high hopes of seeing them together for good some day. This caused her to feel a bit lonely at times, though, for there was nobody special in her own life. George's letters had stopped coming . . . and she found that she didn't really care.

One evening, when she and Sybil had been living in their neat little flat for over a year, there was a knock at the door.

Viney gasped when she saw who their visitor was.

'Tom Russell! What on earth are you doing here? I thought you were still in London!'

'Not for much longer. Aren't you going to invite me in?'

When he was sitting down with a mug of tea in his hand, he told her that he was coming to Llanidris to take over from old Dr Foy, who was retiring.

'I've always liked this part of the world. I've saved up and I can afford to buy the practice.'

'But how did you know it was for sale? Was it advertised in some medical journal?'

Viney missed the wink Sybil gave him.

'Oh, I have my sources,' he grinned, and all at once the world seemed brighter, the sky seemed clearer, and Viney's heart began to sing.

# THE END